W9-BFL-332

c.1

F
K

Kassem, Lou

Listen for Rachel

$11.95

DATE			

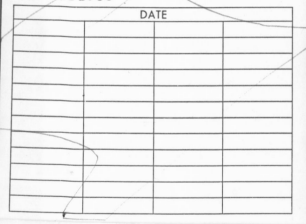

LISTEN FOR RACHEL

"Aye, that it is! Let's make haste, lass. Light's fadin' and Manda will be waiting. Tam's a mite anxious too."

Tam gave truth to those words as he leaped forward across the stream and up the trail at a gallop. Bess was not to be outdone. She took off as fast as her short legs and new rider would allow.

Rachel was having a very hard time staying in the saddle. Grandy was far ahead now. Rachel only hoped Bess knew where she was headed and that she arrived with Rachel aboard—in whatever manner.

"Slow down, Bess, slow *down!*" Rachel yelled as she leaned forward clutching Bess's mane. Her feet came out of the stirrups and she held on by sheer determination.

Suddenly Bess came to an abrupt halt. Rachel went flying over Bess's head. She landed in a heap at the feet of a small woman who looked like an older version of her own mother.

"Ah, Rachel, what a way to be comin' home. Are you hurt anywhere?" The woman bent down to examine her and help her up.

Rachel suddenly thought how funny she must look and started laughing through her tears. "No, ma'am, except for aching in every bone in my body, I'm fine."

"Rachel, this is your grandmother. Manda, the lass who just came flying to meet you is Miss Rachel Sutton. Time somebody remembered some manners 'round here." Jonathan's eyes twinkled with mischief now that he saw Rachel wasn't hurt.

"Manners! You ought to teach that Bess some manners!" Rachel stormed.

"Well, now Rachel," Grandy drawled, "the next time you want Bess to stop . . . try pulling *back* on the reins and

Your Uncle Roscoe and his family live 'bout half a mile on one side of us. Your Uncle Lem and his brood live about two miles on the other side. They're our closest neighbors. Our place is called Carder's Cove 'cause it's tucked up in a little valley with mountains on three sides. We farm some, raise a few cattle, and breed and train a few horses—like Tam, here."

"And Bess?"

"Well, Bess is more of a family horse. We don't use her as breed stock. For all that, she's a good little mare."

"Are there any girls my age, Grandy?"

"Mary Ann is 'bout your age, I reckon. She's Lem's girl. You and Mary Ann are our only granddaughters. Now, Roscoe has three boys and Lem has two. So there are plenty of young folks for you to visit with."

The day wore on. The pace was a steady walk or an easy trot that covered a deceptive number of miles. Then at last, as the light began to fade, they came out of the forest into a valley with a clear, frothy stream racing through it.

The sight of this sheltered valley in the setting sun took Rachel's breath away.

"Little Stoney, Rachel. Only a mile or so to home. This is Carder land—from right here clear back to the mountains." Pride and pleasure put a special glow in Jonathan's voice.

"And the mountains, Grandy, who do they belong to?"

"Mountains belong to God, Rachel." Jonathan's voice was serious now. "Mountains are there to remind us of God's majesty, steadfastness, and protection."

Rachel looked once more at the valley protected on three sides by God's mountains, watered by the clear stream, and cooled by the green forest. "It's beautiful, Grandy. Truly beautiful."

she was afraid she'd fall off. But Grandfather seemed happier by the minute. He and Tam melted together into one easy rhythm. Rachel relaxed and tried to fit her movements to Bess's. It worked! And Bess apparently felt better about her rider.

Tam began to move at a faster clip. Bess was having trouble keeping up. "Easy on, Tam." Grandfather spoke sharply. "Bess's legs aren't as long as yours." Tam's ears flicked back and he obediently slowed his pace.

Rachel was amazed. "Does he understand everything you say to him?"

"Purty near. He's right smart but just a mite headstrong, aren't you, Tam?" For an answer Tam tossed his head and nickered.

Rachel laughed. "I really do think he understands you."

They rode on in a friendly silence. Rachel saw only a few farms along the river road and fewer houses. The country was sparsely settled, it seemed.

"Grandfather, tell me about your house. Who lives there? Is it a settlement? Do you have lots of neighbors?"

Jonathan looked at her curiously for a moment. "Did your mother not tell you about her home, Rachel?" he asked softly.

Rachel shook her head and said thoughtfully, "No, it made her sad when I asked questions about when she was little. I-I think she must have loved this place very much. Leaving it made her sad. So, I didn't ask questions . . . Mama wasn't sad often," she added a trifle defiantly.

Jonathan cleared his throat. Something seemed to have gotten stuck in it. After a minute or so he said, "Well, first off, Rachel, most of the young'uns call me 'Grandy,' not Grandfather. And your grandmother is 'Manda' to just about everybody. Just her and me at the home place now.

8

"There's a room right back through there, Miss Rachel. You can freshen up and change if you've a mind to," Mr. Tipton said.

"Thank you." Rachel took the bundle of clothes and went to the room Mr. Tipton had pointed out.

She washed off the travel dust with pleasure. Her grandmother had sent her a soft blue homespun shirt and a pair of tan homespun britches. She had never worn boy's britches in her life. Still, they were comfortable, and should do very well if she were going to be on a horse all day.

Outside, tied to the hitching post, were two impatient horses. One horse was huge—solid black, except for a long white forelock and mane. The other horse was a shaggy brown-and-white mare, much smaller and wider.

The black horse whinnied and danced as Rachel and Jonathan approached.

"Easy, Tam, easy." Jonathan greeted the horse like a long lost friend. "Missed me, did you? Easy, now. Soon be on our way home, Tam. Rachel, this is Tam O'Shanter. He thinks he's king of Carder's Cove. That little mare is Bess. She's sturdy and gentle as a lamb. She'll take good care of you, won't you, Bess? Here, let me give you a leg up."

Before she knew what had happened Rachel was astride Bess. Goodness, she thought, whatever made me think Bess was small?

Jonathan handed her the reins and quickly mounted Tam. "Just hold the reins and fall in behind me, Rachel. You happen to be up our way, Hugh, stop in an' visit."

"Be sure to, Jonathan. Say howdy to the Missus."

"Good day, Mr. Tipton," Rachel said.

Tam could wait no longer. He started off at a brisk trot. Bess turned and followed him.

At first Rachel was frightened. They were going so fast

A man came out of the store. "Howdy, Jonathan. Back are you?"

"Howdy, Hugh. I'm back. This lass is my granddaughter, Rachel *Sutton*." Jonathan emphasized Rachel's last name ever so slightly as he nudged her forward. "Rachel, this is Mr. Hugh Tipton—runs the store, post office, and stables."

Rachel dropped Mr. Tipton a curtsy, and said primly, "Good afternoon, Mr. Tipton."

Startled by the curtsy, Mr. Tipton managed to give Rachel a quick bow. "Good afternoon to you, Miss Rachel. Welcome to our settlement."

"Enough of this fancy-prancy, Hugh," Grandfather said a bit gruffly. "Have you got the satchel I left and my horses?"

"Now where would I be letting your horses and belongin's go, Jonathan? Come along in the store. Rest a spell whilst I fetch your things."

Rachel followed the two men into the dimly lit store. Once her eyes adjusted to the light, she saw the store was packed floor to ceiling with a variety of goods. Her nose was assailed with a whole range of smells—sweet, sour, tangy, spicy, leathery, old and new. She liked it.

"Rachel, you look like a hound dog sniffin' the trail of a fox," her grandfather said.

"I like your store, Mr. Tipton. It smells—well—like everything good rolled into one big ball."

Mr. Tipton laughed. "So it does, Miss Rachel. So it does!"

Jonathan Carder was rummaging through the satchel Hugh Tipton had given him. "Here, Rachel, your grandmother sent along these clothes for you to wear on the trip home."

"Almost where, Grandfather? Do we have to ride in another coach?" After days of traveling, Rachel dreaded the thought.

Grandfather's eyes twinkled. "Almost to the Watauga Settlement, lass. No more coaches. From there we go on horseback." Noticing the expression in Rachel's eyes, he asked, "You do ride, lass?"

"A-a little, Grandfather. I rode a pony once. Papa held the reins for me."

The other passengers chuckled. But Grandfather said, "You'll be fine, Rachel. Won't take any time for you to get the hang of it. After all, you are a Carder."

Suddenly Rachel's temper flared. "I am not a Carder! My name is Rachel Amanda Sutton."

Surprised by her own outburst, she sat back on the swaying seat with a defiant set to her shoulders.

For a moment, Jonathan Carder's eyes flashed with an icy blue anger. Just as quickly they filled with laughter. "You are one-half Carder, Rachel," he said.

Rachel was spared a reply as the coach lurched to a final stop and the passengers began to tumble out. She was the last one to dismount. While Grandfather removed the satchels from the top of the coach, she surveyed her new surroundings.

There were less than a dozen board or log buildings scattered around in a semicircle. The one the coach had stopped in front of had a sign over the door: TIPTON GENERAL STORE. Rachel couldn't tell what most of the other buildings were, except for the church and the stables at the far end of the semicircle. The Watauga Settlement was bounded on one end by the small river they had just crossed and on the other by a huge mountain.

"I am Jonathan Carder, your grandfather. I come to take you home, Rachel," he said. "Are you packed and ready then?"

Six feet tall and ramrod straight, her grandfather was rather intimidating. "I'm ready," Rachel had answered. And here she was, in a stagecoach with her grandfather, journeying toward the mountains.

Rachel groaned as the coach hit another rut and jolted her back into the present.

"Are you all right, lass?"

"I'm fine, Grandfather," Rachel replied, and turned her face to the window so he couldn't see the tears that threatened.

When she turned back again, she found her grandfather staring at her.

"You look like a banty hen in moltin' season, lass. Are you not feelin' well?" he asked.

"I'm fine," Rachel replied with a faint smile.

"We'll soon be stopping. A bit of food and rest will perk you up right smart."

"Yes, sir."

"Did you notice, lass, the air's a mite cooler and fresher now we're in the mountains?"

Rachel nodded.

"Cain't get thar too soon fer me!" said one of the passengers. "These hyar coaches ain't fit fer man nor beast." There were murmurs of assent from the other two passengers. Then everyone settled back into as comfortable positions as were possible on the jolting coach.

Before long, Rachel felt the horses quicken their pace. Grandfather also noticed the change. "Horses smell food and water. We're almost there."

1

Rachel hadn't believed it at first. It didn't seem possible. One day you were a family. The next day you were all alone.

Two months ago her parents had died, trying to save their store from the blazing inferno that had engulfed an entire section of River Road. Their sacrifice had been in vain. Nothing remained of Sutton's Emporium.

The searing pain and wild grief Rachel felt had gradually subsided into a constant dull ache. Kind neighbors who took her in had gotten in touch with her grandparents. She didn't know much about her kin back in the mountains, but they were family.

The small hope she had had that her grandparents would come to Nashville and claim her had almost faded when, without warning, Grandfather Carder appeared.

He was a stern old man dressed in a dusty black homespun suit. His tan, weathered face was dominated by a pair of deep blue eyes. He wasted no time in small talk.

LISTEN FOR RACHEL

Dedicated to my four daughters who, like Rachel, are imbued with an indomitable spirit.

Margaret K. McElderry Books
Macmillan Publishing Company
866 Third Avenue, New York, N.Y. 10022
Collier Macmillan Canada, Inc.

Composition by Maryland Linotype Composition Company
Baltimore, Maryland
Printed and bound by R. R. Donnelley & Sons Company
Harrisonburg, Virginia
Designed by Christine Kettner

10 9 8 7 6 5 4 3 2 1

Library of Congress Cataloging-in-Publication Data

Kassem, Lou.
    Listen for Rachel.

    "A Margaret K. McElderry book."
    Summary: Moving up into the mountains of
Tennessee introduces Rachel to a possible calling, as
she learns about folk medicine from a local healer,
until the Civil War divides the family loyalties and
brings romance into her life.
    [1. Mountain life—Fiction. 2. Folk medicine—
Fiction. 3. Tennessee—Fiction. 4. United States—
History—Civil War, 1861–1865—Fiction] I. Title.
PZ7.K1545Li 1986   [Fic]   86-8673
ISBN 0-689-50396-2

First Edition

LISTEN FOR RACHEL

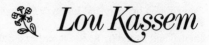 *Lou Kassem*

Margaret K. McElderry Books
NEW YORK

sayin' 'whoa.' Leanin' forward and kicking her whilst yellin' 'slow down' only confuses her."

Manda and Rachel both laughed with Jonathan. Bess and Tam whinnied.

"Come on up to the house, both of you. Supper's been setting on the stove for hours." Manda took Rachel's arm and headed for the log cabin that Rachel had just had time to notice in the clearing.

"I'll see to the horses and be right along." Grandy gave Manda a quick hug and led Bess and Tam away.

Rachel had only a vague memory of her first meal at Carder's Cove. She almost fell asleep in her plate of stew. She did remember being led up some stairs and gentle hands helping her undress. Her last memory was of a soft, soft mattress enfolding her and a light kiss on her cheek.

"Like sleeping on a cloud," she murmured, drifting off to sleep in the feather bed.

"Stay close to the cabin, lass, till you get your bearin's," cautioned Grandy the next morning as he clapped on a battered reed hat and strode out of the cabin.

He need not have worried. The vastness and solitude of the place frightened Rachel. Everywhere she looked all she saw were trees and mountains. No roads. No stores. No people. Only trees, trees, and more trees.

Every morning after he tended the stock in the barn, Grandy disappeared into the thick forest that surrounded the house.

"Where does Grandy go every day?" Rachel asked one morning.

"He's catchin' up on the chores. Got a mite behind with his trip to Nashville," Manda answered with a smile.

"But where does he go to do his chores?" Rachel persisted.

Then Manda understood Rachel's question. "Our cultivated land is scattered—strung out along the valley between the mountains. Every flat piece is farmed or used as pasture for our horses. On a farm there's always work to be done. The whole Carder clan farms this end of the valley. It takes all of us to make it work. We live right good, long as we all do our share. Idle hands are the devil's workshop, you know," Manda explained.

Rachel nodded, thinking the devil was out of luck here. Manda's hands were never idle. She was always busy with sewing, cooking, cleaning, milking, churning, or working in the big garden at the edge of the clearing.

Manda gratefully accepted Rachel's help with jobs that Rachel knew how to do. She patiently taught her any of the other jobs that Rachel wanted to learn.

Grandy came and went like a puff of smoke. Now you saw him, now you didn't.

Somewhat to her surprise, Rachel was enjoying herself. She liked being useful. In one short week, Manda made her feel like a part of the family.

A week slipped by and Rachel hadn't seen another living soul except for Grandy and Manda. She missed the hustle and bustle of having other people about. Pondering this as she helped Manda peel potatoes, she asked, "Have you always lived here, Manda?"

"Lordy me, no, child. Jonathan brought me here as a bride. Only a few years older'n you."

"Weren't you lonely?"

"Oh, maybe a mite at first. Didn't have much time to think about it."

"Where did you live before?"

"Over the mountains yonder—in Virginny. I was a MacDonald before I was a Carder. Scottish on both sides, you see."

"Did you like it right off?"

For a moment Manda stopped to consider. "Why, yes, I suppose I did. Why, Rachel?"

"I—I guess I was thinking about Mama." Rachel gulped. "Why did she leave here?"

Manda looked at Rachel for a long moment. "That bothers you, does it? Well, it's a long story and the past is gone—no changin' it. But, like me comin' here with Jonathan, she had to go where her husband went. Your papa was an 'outlander,' and he took Sarah back to his part of the country. Trouble was, Sarah was our only daughter—apple of her daddy's eye. Jonathan didn't want her to go. Both of them bein' Scots—they had words. . . ."

"And Mama left?"

"Aye, left and never came back or wrote."

"You didn't even know about me?"

"No, Rachel, but I'm glad you're here. It's like havin' Sarah back again."

Rachel smiled her thanks, but something else was bothering her. "Manda, why haven't our relatives come over to visit? I've been here a week now."

Manda looked at Rachel curiously. "Mountain manners, honey. They're givin' you time to settle yourself. Wouldn't be polite to come traipsin' over just to gawk at you."

"You'll meet more'n you can remember come Sunday," Grandy promised as he came in for his noon meal. "Circuit rider's due."

"What's a circuit rider?"

"Preacher who comes by onct a month. We don't have a fancy church so he holds services in the house, barn, or outdoors, depending on the weather or the crowd," Grandy explained.

Rachel was excited about meeting her new aunts, uncles, and cousins but a little nervous, too. Would they like her? Would she like them? She didn't particularly want to be gawked at. She went to bed that night filled with anticipation and a little fear.

"Lord-a-mercy, she looks just like Sarah!"

"No, she don't. She's got Grandy's eyes."

"She looks more like Manda to me!"

"Well, Sarah looked like Manda, Martha. It's plain to see as the nose on your face who Rachel favors," Aunt Rose said, laughing.

Martha grabbed Rachel by the hand. "Let's ask Granny Sharp. She'll be a fair judge."

"Granny Sharp's not here today," Aunt Rose said.

"Who's sick?"

"Folks along Beaver Creek all come down with a stummick sickness, I hear tell. Granny Sharp's got her hands full."

"That's too bad. Granny hates to miss Meeting," Aunt Martha said, letting go of Rachel.

Conversation continued to flow around Rachel as if she weren't there. She wished people would talk to her, not over her head as if she were invisible. And, what was worse, she didn't think she'd ever get all the names and faces put together! In addition to her relatives there were whole families of Hardins, Hyders, Morrells, Renfrews, and Taylors.

When the preacher came, everyone went outside and sat on the ground or on the scattered benches. The preacher stood on the porch and preached for an hour and a half. Afterward, everybody gathered around the long, well-laden tables and filled their plates. The young people, of course, were last.

Someone tapped Rachel on the shoulder. Turning, Rachel saw a boy she was sure she'd met earlier.

"Let's take our plates down by the crick, Rachel. I'm sure tired of this passel o'people."

"Me, too," Rachel said, as she followed him through the crowd.

"I'm Jason, Uncle Roscoe's boy, if you've forgot."

"I'm sorry. I did forget. There are so many people and names to remember," Rachel said, her voice quavering.

"Hey, you'll get us all straight in no time. Don't worry on it."

"Worry on what?" asked the girl who had just joined them, uninvited.

Rachel did remember her. This was Mary Ann, the other granddaughter, Lem's girl. "Hello, Mary Ann. Won't you join us?"

Mary Ann had already seated herself beside Jason. She gave Rachel an unfriendly glance. "Worry on what, Jason?" she asked.

"Nothin' much, Mary Ann. Rachel, here, is having trouble keepin' us all straight."

"Is that what she's about to bawl over?" Mary Ann sneered. "Lordy me, how old did Grandy say she was?"

That did it. Rachel could take no more. Adults could talk over her head but no uppity cousin was going to do it! "Old enough to have some manners—which, obviously, you

15

don't," Rachel said, her eyes flashing fire. "Excuse me, Jason. I find I'm not hungry anymore." So saying, she picked up her plate and marched away.

Jason and Mary Ann just sat and stared at Rachel's stiff, retreating back.

"Well, lah-de-dah! 'I find I'm not hungry anymore,'" Mary Ann mimicked.

Jason started laughing. "You ast for it and you got it, Mary Ann."

"Got what?"

"Your comeuppance, that's what!" Jason got up and ran to catch up with Rachel.

"We'll just see about you, Miss Rachel," Mary Ann muttered to herself as she rose to her feet. "I don't know what I'll do yet, but I'll fix your wagon—just wait and see!"

Rachel was too busy the rest of the afternoon to worry about her set-to with Mary Ann. Manda asked her to help pack up the extra food. Then she helped with the dishes. And, finally, she minded the younger neighbor children while the preacher gave one last sermon.

Shadows were filling the valley when everyone started homeward.

Rachel stood on the front porch with Manda and Grandy and once more shook everyone's hand. Everyone's except Mary Ann's. Mary Ann didn't come by at all. She sat in the wagon and waited impatiently for her family.

Rachel's face felt stiff from smiling and she was very tired. What was worse, she wasn't sure how everyone felt about her. Several people had commented on her fancy clothes and her different way of speaking. For certain, Mary Ann didn't care for her new cousin!

The last wagon was pulling out when a figure tumbled from the tailgate and came running toward the porch.

"Forget something, Jason?" Grandy called, laughing at the dust covered boy.

"No, I recollected something," Jason replied, brushing some of the dust away. "I recollected I didn't get a piece of Manda's blackberry pie afore it was gobbled up."

"Was it worth tearing your trousers to tell us that?" Manda asked.

Jason dismissed the jagged rip with a shrug. "You make the best blackberry pies in the whole world, Manda."

"Well, you tore your Sunday britches for nothing, Jason," Manda said, looking pleased anyway. "I don't have airy piece left."

Jason gave Rachel a big wink. "That's what I figured! How 'bout me and Rachel going pickin' tomorrow? Would you bake us a pie? I know a place with blackberries big as walnuts!"

"With berries of that size you'll only need a few, Jason. You take Mary Ann and Rachel along and there'll be pie for th' whole clan," Grandy said.

"Hoo-eee! I'll be by for you early in the mornin' then, Rachel. Just you wait till you taste Manda's blackberry cobbler!"

"I'll be waiting," Rachel promised, laughing. She felt she'd found her first friend.

2

"Hoo-ho-oo, Ra-ch-el! Hoo, hoo-o-o-o-."

Rachel ran to her window and peered out. "Jason, is that you? Hush now, you'll wake everyone up. I'll be right down."

Hurriedly she threw on her clothes and raced downstairs as quietly as she could.

In the kitchen she found Manda packing a lunch pail and Jason eating a cold ham biscuit with a mug of milk.

"You're pretty quick—for a girl. Sit down and have a bite 'fore we go," Jason said, reaching for another biscuit.

"I'm sorry you had to get up so early, Manda."

"Who could sleep with that wolf howlin' outside? Jonathan went for his shotgun. Next time that wolf better watch out or his hide will be hangin' over the fireplace," Manda said seriously.

"Aw, Manda, you all knowed it was me. I don't sound like no wolf!" Jason tried to look downcast and hurt.

Rachel giggled at his silly face. "Where's Mary Ann?"

Jason squirmed in his seat a little before answering. "Well, I went over for her before I come over here. She sure didn't seem too happy 'bout going with us. So I just came on by myself," Jason said innocently.

"Musta been dark when you stopped by her house," Manda said.

"Not quite. It was gettin' light," Jason answered defensively.

"Never mind, you two can get enough berries for all of us. Here's your lunch. Now Jason, don't eat it all before you get there. I 'spect you've already had two breakfasts."

"I told you I was a growin' boy." Jason laughed. "Come on, Rachel, let's go. You carry the lunch. It'll be safer." He picked up two lard buckets and dashed out the door.

"Be careful, now. Be back before sundown, Jason," Manda called after them.

The two figures were soon swallowed up in the dark forest behind the cabin. Little trails branched off in all directions. Jason knew just where he was going. Rachel was glad. She'd never explored this far from the cabin.

"Where are we going to find the blackberries, Jason?"

"High Meadows. You can find blackberries all around. But the biggest and best are up there. It's a long hike, but it'll be worth it."

The trails went mostly up. Rachel had always thought there was only one big mountain behind the house. She discovered that instead of one mountain, it was a series of mountains each a little higher than the one before. The leaves of the trees made them merge into one when you looked up at them.

Rachel and Jason were a good team. Rachel was curious

19

about everything and asked questions constantly. Jason knew every plant, animal, and trail in these woods and loved explaining about them. He showed her the difference between the oak, maple, sycamore, hickory, and walnut trees.

Rachel stopped to catch her breath after a particularly steep hill. Nestled at her feet were patches of deep purple flowers. She stooped to pick a bouquet.

"Stop!" shouted Jason.

Rachel jumped back. "Why? What's wrong?"

"Almost put your hand down in poison ivy. That's what. You'd be itching all over by night."

"Which is poison ivy?"

"That three-leafed plant growin' all through there. Remember the ole rhyme: 'Leaves of three, let it be!' Rested now? Only one more big climb."

The sun had come up full in the sky now. And, even in the leaf sheltered forest, it was growing hot. Rachel's clothes were damp with sweat and she was panting like one of Grandy's hound dogs. The lunch bucket had also gotten considerably heavier.

"Hurry up, Rachel. We're almost there. I've got a surprise for you."

Jason wasn't even breathing hard. But he stopped and waited for Rachel to catch up.

"Close your eyes, now. I'll lead you the rest of the way. This is my favorite place in the world."

When Rachel opened her eyes she could see why. They were on the very top of a mountain in a large meadow filled with lush green grass and dozens of varieties of flowers. In the very center of the meadow was a lake of crystal clear blue water.

"Open your mouth."

Rachel did. Jason plopped in a huge sweet blackberry.

"Was it worth the hike?"

"Oh, yes, Jason," Rachel whispered, still awed by the fairy-tale appearance of the meadow.

Jason was busy picking huge blackberries and stuffing them in his mouth.

The blackberry bushes circled the whole meadow next to the forest. They *were* the biggest berries Rachel had ever seen.

"Let's go for a swim. Cool us off." Jason raced away for the lake. He stopped on the grassy edge just long enough to remove his shoes. Then, he dived head first into the water, clothes and all.

Rachel came along more slowly. The water looked cool and inviting.

"Come on, Rachel. Our clothes will be dry before we start home."

"I can't swim, Jason. But I'd like to cool my feet."

The water was so icy cold it took her breath away. But it was refreshing and so clear she could see right to the bottom.

Afterwards, they sat in the long sweet grass and let the sun dry them.

Jason insisted it was time to eat.

"How do you know?"

" 'Cause my stomach is making fearsome noises—and the sun's almost directly overhead."

Rachel had to admit she was a trifle hungry herself. She got the lunch pail and spread out Manda's and Aunt Rose's contributions.

"Rachel, I've told you about things here. Now it's your turn. Tell me about Nashville. Do you miss it much? Tell me all about it. I never been farther than the Watauga Settlement."

So, while they ate, Rachel told Jason all about the place that had been her home.

"I miss Mama and Papa most. But, no, I don't miss Nashville much. Nashville's a big place with lots of people and houses. Lots of stores and churches and schools. It's built on both sides of the Cumberland River. Big steamboats carry all kinds of things up and downriver. You ever see a steamboat, Jason?"

Jason shook his head.

"They're real big—bigger than Grandy's barn. They have loud whistles that you can hear for miles. Papa used to know the sound of each boat's whistle. 'There's Captain Maynard on the *River Queen*'—or, 'That's *Lucky Lady*,' he'd say. He used to take me down to the docks sometimes." Rachel's voice trailed away into silence as she remembered those times.

"What was it your pa did? I don't remember anybody sayin'."

"Papa used to say he was a finder. If folks had something they wanted to sell he'd find a buyer, or if they wanted to buy something he'd find it for them. That was when I was little. We moved about a lot. Then, when Papa was ready to settle down, we started our own store."

"Like Mr. Tipton's?"

"Oh, much grander than that! Papa said Sutton's Emporium would be the biggest and grandest store in Nashville. It would have been, too!" Rachel said fiercely, trying to hold back the tears that stung the backs of her eyes.

"I bet it would!" Jason agreed stoutly. "I sure would like to see a store bigger than Tipton's. What did you do in Nashville?"

"Went to school mostly. Helped Mama around the

house when she'd let me. She said there wasn't enough work for one, much less two."

Jason looked at Rachel with wide-eyed disbelief. "Didn't you have a garden? Chickens? A cow?"

"Not in a city, Jason." Rachel laughed.

"How'd you get your milk, eggs, and vegetables then?"

"Farmers living out in the country came into town to sell their produce."

"What if they didn't come one day? What would you do then?"

"Do without."

"I don't think I'd like livin' in a city, dependin' on someone else to feed me," declared Jason, popping the last sandwich in his mouth.

"Sometimes I don't think Mama liked it either. She complained that the vegetables and eggs weren't always fresh. She wanted to dig up our back lot for a garden but Papa wouldn't let her. Papa said that ladies in our position didn't slave away in the hot sun."

"What was your position?" Jason asked curiously.

"Papa intended us to be one of the leading families in Nashville within one year. We were going to build a big house on the hill and have servants and everything! I was even going to have a 'coming-out' ball when I was eighteen."

"Comin' out o' where?"

Rachel couldn't help laughing at Jason's puzzled expression. "Why, I guess, it's a way of announcing that you are out of your childhood and eligible to marry. You have a grand ball and are presented to society."

"Well, if that don't beat all!" Jason exclaimed. "Up here if a girl is eighteen and not married she sure don't go around announcin' it. Most likely she's ugly as a toad, or lazy or ornery, if she ain't bespoken by then. Things sure are different in the city."

"You can say that again!"

"Why? I said it onct," Jason queried. Then looking at Rachel's face which wore both an amused and puzzled look he said brightly, "Don't worry, Rachel. As pretty as you are, you'll have beaus as thick as fleas on a hound dog. Now— let's pick us some dessert. I'm almost full."

Rachel blushed at Jason's strange compliment. "We'd better pick Manda some blackberries while we're at it," she said.

"Right! Can't make a blackberry cobbler without black-berries. Every third berry goes home!"

Soon, both Rachel's and Jason's mouths and hands were dyed a rich purple. The lard buckets were filling up fast, in spite of the unequal treatment they were getting.

At sunset Manda saw the two weary but happy berry pickers come out of the woods.

"Have supper and stay the night with us, Jason. I'll fix your pie tomorrow," Manda invited as she took the brim-ming buckets of berries.

"You don't have to ask twice," Jason said, planting a berry-stained kiss on Manda's forehead.

It was another hot, clear, windless day. Although they had had several evening showers, it wasn't enough rain "to grow weeds, much less a garden," as Grandy said.

Rachel was trying to remedy that situation by carrying water from the creek to Manda's garden patch. She was finding it very hot and tiring work. Unlike Manda, who went barefoot every day except Sunday, Rachel found that going unshod had its problems. Her tender feet found every sharp stone and briar in the area. Manda said her feet would toughen up soon.

She sat down on the creek bank and dangled her bruised feet in the clear, cool water. It was strange how much her life had changed in these few short weeks . . . even to going barefoot. Papa would never let her go without shoes, even around the house. He said ladies didn't go unshod because it made their feet too big to fit into their dance slippers.

"I don't think I need worry about dance slippers up here." Rachel smiled, surveying the solid, two-story log house, the well-kept barn, and the long, neat rows of the garden.

It certainly was different! Different, but not bad. Actually, it was fun being a useful part of a family, even if she couldn't do some tasks. And Manda was awfully patient with her, showing her how to churn for butter and how to collect eggs from a nest when the hen was still on it. And, given more practice, she knew she could milk Bessy without getting kicked!

"Howdy, Rachel."

Surprised, Rachel turned to find Mary Ann smiling down at her.

"Hello, Mary Ann. I didn't hear you come up. Sit down and cool off. Sure is hot, isn't it?" Rachel said with cautious friendliness.

Mary Ann sat down beside her as if nothing had ever happened between them.

"Yep, it's hot aw right. I had to do the same as you for our garden yesterday. We need rain bad."

"We could use it."

"Manda said you was about finished. You want to go pick some berries with me? Seein' as how I didn't go along last time."

Rachel didn't know exactly what to answer.

"It's too hot to climb all the way to High Meadow, isn't it?"

"Oh, we wouldn't go up there. There's lots of other places just as good, no matter what Jason says! 'Course if you don't want to go with me. . . ."

"Of course I do. Those blackberry cobblers of Manda's are worth being a little hot over. Let me get my shoes and we'll go."

The trails Mary Ann took were in a different direction and not nearly as steep as the trail to High Meadow. The woods were cooler but Rachel was still sticky hot.

Mary Ann was a very different companion from Jason. She chattered endlessly about clothes, fashions, and her different beaus.

"Did you have a steady beau before you left Nashville?"

"Goodness me, no! Mama said I was too young to be thinking seriously about boys. Of course, Laura Lee and I did have some special fellows we liked in school."

"Too young?" Mary Ann was shocked. "You're almost fifteen! Why in a few more years you'll be an old maid. I already got my eye on a likely fellow. He's been eyin' me, too." Mary Ann laughed rather smugly.

"Lots of apples on the tree. I'll take my time in pickin' one, I guess. How much farther, Mary Ann?"

"Only a little ways more—right over this hill."

When they reached the berry patch, Rachel could see it was pretty well picked over. Besides, the berries weren't nearly as big as the ones she and Jason had picked.

"The birds and bears have been into these, I'll wager," Mary Ann said.

"Something has, that's for sure."

"Just means we'll have to work harder. I know—I'll work this side of the hill and around. You go round to the other side. By the time we meet our buckets will be full."

Rachel sighed. She wasn't too happy about the whole idea. But, as long as she was here, she might as well get some berries.

"All right, Mary Ann. See you on the other side of the hill." Rachel set off and soon lost sight of Mary Ann.

Rachel's berry bucket wasn't filling up very fast. The only good berries left were the ones in the middle of the patch. In order to get those Rachel spent a good deal of time on her hands and knees. She was also collecting numerous scratches and cuts.

Stopping to rest and inspect her latest scratch, Rachel suddenly felt frightened.

"What's wrong?" She looked all around searchingly. Nothing had changed. Still she was uneasy. Something was different. What was it? Rachel stood very still trying to calm her fear. She almost called out to Mary Ann, but thought better of it. Mary Ann would call her a baby. No, she would figure it out by herself! Rachel made herself stand very still and think.

Then it came to her. It was too quiet! No birds sang, no bees buzzed, no wind rustled the leaves of the trees. The meadow that was usually filled with a variety of sounds of animals and insects was deadly quiet—and deserted, too. Rachel turned in a circle, looking all around her. No birds, no bees, not even a butterfly. And it was getting dark! Angry dark gray clouds were moving rapidly over the mountains, filling the whole sky.

Rachel panicked. She dropped her bucket and ran, calling for Mary Ann. Stumbling and almost falling, she came around the other side of the hill. "Mary Ann, where are you? Mary Ann?"

Mary Ann was nowhere to be seen. She had vanished along with the bees and birds.

Thunder rolled and crashed over and around and through the mountains. The ground shook beneath Rachel's feet. The dark clouds burst open sending a river of rain down on the meadow and Rachel.

Lightning zigzagged across the sky. A bolt crashed down

and hopped, skipped, and jumped across the meadow toward Rachel.

Rachel ran.

Mary Ann was halfway home when the storm struck. She had been so busy rehearsing the story she was going to tell that she hadn't noticed the change in the weather.

Her plan was simple. She would arrive at Grandy's, out of breath and worried. In spite of all her warnings, she would say, Rachel had wandered off on her own. She had called and searched but couldn't find Rachel. Everyone would have to stop what they were doing and go out and look for the "little baby" city girl. Grandy would be real mad at Rachel. He hated to have to stop when he was training his horses. Besides, he didn't have much use for people who didn't listen to good sense. Maybe they would decide Rachel didn't belong here and send her back to Nashville.

The sudden fierce storm changed all Mary Ann's plans. Now, she was frightened. She knew only too well how bad these sudden storms could be. Small streams could turn into raging torrents and become impassable. Trees would be uprooted and often there were landslides in the mountains.

With thunder and lightning crashing all around her, Mary Ann ran for her life.

Manda was waiting in the cabin door when Mary Ann stumbled in, sobbing and shaking with fear and cold.

"Where's Rachel?" Manda was busy wrapping Mary Ann in a quilt. "She right behind you? Jonathan, look to see if she's comin'. Hush now, child! You're safe and snug as a bug in a rug."

"Don't see her anywhere, Manda," Jonathan's eyes showed his concern but his voice was calm. "Mary Ann, stop cryin' and tell us where Rachel is."

Mary Ann couldn't seem to stop crying. She realized now that what she had done might cost her cousin's life. Still, she couldn't admit what she had done. Grandy and Manda wouldn't love her anymore, for sure.

"R-R-Rachel wan-dered off!" Mary Ann said between sobs. "I was comin' for h-help when the-the storm b-roke."

"Where were you?" Grandy was putting on his slicker and boots. "Think now, Mary Ann. Where did you last see Rachel?"

"B-Buffalo Meadow—south side—I think."

"I'll ride to Lem's. We'll round up all the men we can. Start searchin' at first light. We'll find her. Don't worry, Manda, me and the boys will find her." Jonathan picked up his rifle, slammed on his hat, and set off in the storm.

4

Rachel ran until she was exhausted. She lost count of how many times she fell, got up, ran, fell and got up and ran again. Finally, she fell and hadn't the strength to get up again. It was so dark that she couldn't see her hand held up before her face. Even under the trees the rain was heavy. Rachel was drenched.

"I've got to find shelter. I'm lost and I'm too tired to find my way home. Besides, it's so dark I can't see anything anyway."

Rachel began to crawl forward. She soon realized she was going uphill. Her forward progress was blocked by a large boulder. She started to crawl around it. She tried to stand but the hill was slippery with rain and she fell to her knees again. Crawling seemed to be her best mode of travel.

This was the way she discovered the cave. If she had been walking, she would have missed the narrow crevice between two boulders.

Rachel crawled into the opening and collapsed on the dry floor. She was shaking as much with terror as with cold.

It seemed to her that she was being pursued by an angry God, hurling lightning bolts and buckets of rain at her. "What have I done wrong?" she whispered.

There was no answer—only the sound of rain drumming down on the trees and the distant rumble of thunder.

"Well, I can't just lie here like a knot on a log or I'll freeze to death!" So saying, Rachel pushed herself upright and began to feel her way around the cave.

"If I keep moving I won't be so cold. But I'd better be careful. No telling how big this cave is or who it belongs to."

Rachel discovered the cave wasn't very deep by bumping her head against the back wall.

"I *hate* these mountains!" she cried, as she rubbed the lump on her forehead. She crumpled up in a wet heap against the back wall of the cave. Gradually, her teeth stopped chattering and, later, she drifted into a troubled sleep.

A giant stared Rachel in the face. He was huge—filling up the whole entrance to the cave. And he just squatted there and stared at her.

Maybe I'm dreaming. I'll close my eyes and count to ten. When I open them he'll be gone. Rachel closed her eyes and counted.

When she opened her eyes he was still there—watching her. He hadn't moved a muscle.

"Uh-uh—who are you?" Rachel croaked.

"I be Juner. You, Rachel?" His voice was low and soft, almost childish.

Rachel nodded.

"Good! You hurt?" Juner eyed Rachel's assorted cuts, bruises, and scrapes.

Rachel looked herself over. She was a mess! Her clothes

were a damp collection of rags and she was scraped and cut all over.

"Nothing serious, Juner. Soap and water will fix most of it. And some dry clothes. Were you looking for me? How did you find me?"

Juner smiled with childish pride. "Granny Sharp says 'Juner, go find Rachel.' I did. Juner found you."

"You sure did." Rachel stood up to test her legs. She was stiff and sore but she could walk. "Is the storm over? Can we go back to Carder's Cove now?"

Juner grinned at her. "Granny said I knowed the mountains best and could find you. And I did. She said, 'Bring her home, Juner.' I gonner do just what Granny says." Juner turned and began to squeeze himself through the narrow cave entrance.

Rachel followed. Outside she realized how big Juner really was. He was well over six feet tall with a body like a sturdy tree trunk. Juner was a big man. Except, Rachel realized, he wasn't really a man—more like an overgrown boy.

"Let's go. Juner hongry. You hongry?"

Rachel laughed. The world looked fresh and newly washed. The sky was blue, birds sang. And Rachel's stomach rumbled. She *was* hungry.

"Why you laughin'?" Juner scowled at her.

"Why, because I'm happy and hungry, Juner. Last night I was so scared and cold and lost. Now all I'm worried about is my stomach rumbling. Isn't that funny?"

Juner's face cleared. "Yeah, that's right funny. Juner's stomach makes funny noises too. Let's go." He took off down the mountain at a rapid clip.

"Wait! Wait up, Juner! I can't go so fast."

Juner stopped abruptly. He turned and scowled at

Rachel, puzzled. Then his face brightened. "You just a little 'un, Rachel. Juner give you a piggyback. We be home in two shakes of a sheep's tail." He turned around and squatted down. "Hop on, Rachel."

Rachel hesitated only a moment. She didn't care how silly it looked if it would get her home to Manda and Grandy sooner.

Rachel threw her arms around Juner's neck. Juner rose as though she wasn't there and trotted off down the mountain.

"Tell me if you get tired, Juner."

"Juner's strong. Don't git tard much. Gits hongry though." Juner slipped as silently through the wet forest as a deer.

"Juner, are other folks out looking for me?"

"Yes, ma'am. All the Carders and neighbors is out looking. But Juner found you."

Rachel thought for a moment. "Won't they go on looking for me? How will they know you've found me?"

Juner stopped. "Juner forgot. Everybody fire three shots if they find you."

"Then, fire three shots."

"Cain't. Granny won't let me have a gun. Juner was suppose to holler. I forgot."

"It hasn't been long, Juner. No one will be mad at you." Rachel sensed how uneasy he was.

"Juner better do it now." He bent down to let Rachel slide off his back. Then he threw back his head and gave a bloodcurdling yell. "Ai-ayh-ayh-a-ree-ah." He gave the strange yell three times and waited. Far off in the distance three shots were fired. And like a distant echo came three more shots.

"They know now. Hop on, Rachel, Juner take you on home."

"Goodness me! Where did you learn that—that yell? I never heard anything like that."

"That be a hunter's yell. Come from the Indians to the mountain men, I 'spect."

Mounted on her strange steed, Rachel found time to admire the wild beauty of the mountains and forest.

"It's so beautiful up here. I don't know why I was so frightened."

"You was alone. Bein' alone is scary. I was awful scairt livin' alone up hyar." Juner's voice still held an echo of remembered fear.

"You lived up here? All alone? When?"

" 'Fore I came to live with Granny Sharp. Mr. Carder, he found me livin' up hyar. 'Bout half starved, I wuz. Granny took me in. She be a good yarb doctor. I come along just in time to help her. That's what Granny says."

Rachel heard the pride in the way Juner said he helped Granny Sharp. She was beginning to understand this gentle giant who had rescued her.

"What do you help Granny Sharp do, Juner?"

"Gather yarbs for medicine. She be getting too old to bend down an' dig roots an' all. I kin do that good. Juner is strong."

By now Rachel had figured out that "yarbs" were herbs that Granny Sharp made into medicines. She hadn't met Granny Sharp but decided that she would certainly do just that very soon.

Rachel began to notice places that seemed familiar.

"Juner, are we near home?"

"Be there in two shakes of a sheep's tail."

"Please put me down, Juner. I want to walk the rest of the way."

"Shure, Miss Rachel."

And so Rachel walked the rest of the way home.

The clearing was filled with neighbors and family. A mighty cheer went up when she limped into the yard.

Manda and another woman rushed to catch Rachel as she stumbled. Holding her between them, they helped her upstairs to her own room.

"This is Granny Sharp," Manda said as she helped Rachel out of her damp clothes. "She'll tend you whilst I fetch you some food and herb tea."

"I don't want anything to eat right now," Rachel mumbled from under the flannel gown Granny Sharp was slipping over her head. Suddenly her body was cold and full of shivers again.

"Just some hot tea, Manda," Granny Sharp advised. She began washing Rachel's cuts while probing gently for broken bones. "You hurt anywheres particular, Rachel?"

"No, ma'am. All over."

Granny Sharp gave her an understanding smile. "You're banged up right smart. Nothing serious. But you'll be sore for a few days. This salve will help the healing."

Rachel tried to hold her shaking body still while Granny Sharp tenderly rubbed a cool, white salve on her cuts.

"Being lost in these lonesome mountains is scary," Granny Sharp said. "Why, sometimes on a dark night even I get turned around and panicky. And I've lived here better'n forty years."

Rachel smiled gratefully. She liked this small, wiry woman with her gentle hands and comforting voice. "I sure was scared."

Granny Sharp helped her under the covers. "Anybody with the sense God gave a goose would ha' been frightened!"

Manda reappeared with a cup of steaming tea. Granny Sharp added a pinch of something, then handed the cup to Rachel. "Drink this and you'll drop right off. Sleep's better'n any medicine I can make."

Rachel drank the hot brew. Already her eyes felt heavy. But something was bothering her. "Is Mary Ann all right?"

Manda and Granny Sharp exchanged glances.

"Mary Ann's just fine," Manda replied.

"You go on to sleep," Granny Sharp advised. "You can talk later."

"Please thank Juner for finding me," Rachel mumbled.

"I will. Sleep well, Rachel," Granny Sharp said.

Rachel closed her eyes. The image of Granny Sharp's ageless, concerned face bending over her was her last conscious memory. It was very comforting.

5

"Lord-a-mercy, I never saw so many cuts, scratches, and bruises!" Manda said, looking at Rachel the next morning with a critical eye. "You're mighty lucky you didn't break an arm or leg, lass. Here, sit and eat some breakfast."

"It smells good, Manda." Rachel sat down and quickly began to eat the hot cakes and sausage Manda set before her. "Tastes good, too. I didn't eat much yesterday—too excited and tired, I guess. Are those eggs for me?"

Manda pretended to look for someone under the table. "I don't see anyone else hereabouts. Must be you I fixed 'em for," she said with a laugh.

"Reckon I'm like Juner—always 'hongry'!" Rachel helped herself to eggs and grits. "Tell me about Juner, Manda. How did he get a name like Juner?"

"It's a sad tale—fact is, we can only guess about the first of it. Reckon some family traveling through either lost or left behind their boy. Guess you could tell that Juner's not too bright. Anyways, 'bout ten years ago your Grandy was up in the mountains looking for an old cougar that been after the lambs and he come across this half-wild, half-starved young'un livin' in a cave. He brought him down to Granny Sharp. She tended and tamed him. Poor thing, didn't know his name or anything about his folks. So, since it was June when he came to her, Granny called him Juner."

Tears had filled Rachel's eyes when Manda finished. "Poor little fellow. All alone up there. Oh, Manda, how could anyone be so cruel?"

"Now, honey, don't fret yourself." Manda came over and hugged her. "Things usually work out for the best. Juner has a home now and someone who loves him. He's a big help to Granny with her herb gathering."

"I-I guess you're right, Manda. Having someone who loves you is the most important thing in the whole world, isn't it?"

"Just about, honey. Now, suppose you tell me about your adventure. How came you to wander off like that?"

"Wander off? Manda, I didn't wander off anywhere! The berries were all picked over, so Mary Ann said we'd split up . . . me on one side of the hill, her on the other. So, we did. All of a sudden it got real quiet. It was really spooky, Manda. The bees and birds and everything just disappeared. Then it got dark." Rachel's eyes glazed over as she remembered the eerie silence and darkness. She shivered. "I got scared and ran around to the other side hollering for Mary Ann. But she had disappeared, too! Then came the thunder and lightning and—and—I don't remember much else. I just ran and ran."

Grandy had come in unnoticed while Rachel was telling her story. He shot a knowing, angry glance at Manda. "Hmm—I thought mayhap we'd not heard the straight of it," he said, clamping his hat back on and turning to go. His whole body bespoke his anger.

"Less said, sooner mended!" Manda cautioned.

Grandy stopped.

No one spoke.

At first, Rachel didn't understand. Then it dawned on her. Her night on the mountain had been no accident! Mary Ann had deliberately run off and left her.

Manda stood between them watching Grandy's tense back and the emotions play across Rachel's face.

Surprise, anger, and, finally, shame were reflected on Rachel's mobile face. She broke the tense silence, as Grandy relaxed and turned around. "I'm sorry I caused so much trouble and worry for everyone. Reckon I'm still an outlander."

"Oh, fiddlesticks!" Manda sputtered. "You may not be mountain born but you're mountain bred—you can never be an outlander. I dare anyone to say different!"

"Now, Miz Manda, don't get *your* tail feathers ruffled!" Grandy chuckled at Manda's outburst.

"Hmpt! Guess you are the only one allowed to have a temper, then," Manda said.

"I've more'n enough for both of us, I allow," Jonathan replied, sheepishly.

"That's so!" But Manda relented with a chuckle.

Jonathan cleared his throat. "Now, Rachel, I been thinkin' that it's high time you learned to ride. If you are about filled up, you can come with me to the south meadow. I'm trainin' some of our horses. Maybe you'd like to pick one for your own?"

Rachel welcomed the idea. "I'm finished. Let's go. Time's a-wasting!"

Down in the south meadow Rachel found her first love. From the string of twelve two year olds, she picked a little strawberry roan with a white star over one eye.

"They're all beautiful, Grandy. But I want the little red one with the star."

"Aye, that's a good choice, Rachel. She's a nice little gal. Why'd you pick her?"

"I like the way she runs—with her head up high. And the way she shines in the sunlight. Like somebody just polished her."

Grandy laughed. "She's all yours. Now we've got to train her. You best help, Rachel. Then she'll be truly your horse."

"Her name's Bright Star."

"Aye. Bright Star suits her fine."

Training Bright Star was hard work. She was a spirited little filly who didn't take too kindly to her loss of freedom.

In the next few days Rachel wound up on the ground more times than she could count. Each time she got up, dusted herself off, and tried again.

Grandy watched and gave advice and encouragement.

The training, both Star's and Rachel's, went on for two weeks before Rachel could ride around the corral with some skill.

"Just keep at it, lass. Use your legs and keep a gentle hand on those reins," Grandy advised one morning. "The rest is up to you. You don't need me anymore. I'm off to the house now."

"I'll try to remember, Grandy," Rachel said, wiping her sweaty forehead on her sleeve. "Tell Manda I'll be along in a little while."

Rachel watched Grandy disappear with long strides into the woods. She was both happy and sad. Happy that he thought she could work on her own. Sad that he wouldn't be spending any more time with her. For the past few weeks, she had felt closer to him than ever before.

Sighing, Rachel gave Star a nudge with her heels and rode through the corral gate. "Come on, Star. Let's get out in the meadow and see how we do today."

From the shadow of the trees, Grandy watched Rachel gallop around the meadow. He smiled a smile of pure satisfaction. Rachel, like himself, was a born rider.

"Show her how to do something—next time she can do it. She takes to horses like a duck to water," Grandy told Manda when he got back to the cabin. "She's got Bright Star eatin' out o' her hand. Pretty soon, she won't need reins. Star will just read her mind."

"Like you and Tam O'Shanter? She's a chip off the old block, eh?"

"Reckon so." Grandy laughed.

The summer days melted into one another like butter on a hot biscuit. Rachel didn't spend all of her time with Bright Star, though she would have liked nothing better. Manda needed her to help put by the vegetables from the garden. And there were always the everyday chores of cooking, cleaning, washing, milking, and egg-gathering. Rachel pitched in and did her share cheerfully.

"Don't see how I managed without you, Rachel," Manda said one morning as they were making kraut and piccalilli.

"Maybe you didn't have to put by so much when I wasn't here. Are we really ever going to eat all of this?"

"Come spring the root cellar will be almost empty. You'll be glad of every bite if we have a long winter."

"Right now I don't ever want to see another head of cabbage." Rachel sighed.

"Halloo, Cabin!"

"Landsakes, who can that be?" Manda wondered. "Run around front and see who it is, Rachel."

Rachel gladly wiped her hands on her apron and went to see who was calling.

A vaguely familiar man sat astride a flop-eared mule and waited to be invited down.

"Mornin', Miss Rachel," he said politely. "Is Jonathan or Miz Manda about?"

"Mornin', Mr. Renfrew," Rachel replied. He was one of the neighbors who had come to welcome her, and his name popped into her mouth as she spoke. "Manda's out back, chopping cabbage. Won't you get down and have a cup of cold water?"

"Don't mind if I do. It's powerful hot today, ain't it?"

"That it is," agreed Rachel, pushing a damp strand of hair from her eyes.

Rachel led Mr. Renfrew to the back stoop and fetched him a dipper of cold water.

Manda and Mr. Renfrew exchanged news of each other's families while Rachel went back to chopping cabbage.

Finally, Mr. Renfrew allowed he'd best get on about his business if Manda could tell him where Jonathan could be found.

"He's over to Lem's, helping put up a shed. You ride on over. They'll be glad of your company," Manda said.

"Yes, ma'am," Mr. Renfrew replied, laughing. " 'Nother pair o' hands is always welcome. Y'all come up an' visit us for a spell—anytime."

"We'll surely do that," Manda replied.

"Thanks for the water, Miss Rachel. It was mighty good," Mr. Renfrew said, clamping his hat on and loping off.

Rachel was puzzled. Mr. Renfrew was only one of the

many visitors who had dropped by to see Grandy since she'd been here.

"Manda, what do all of these people want with Grandy?"

"This and that," Manda replied. "I 'spect Charlie Renfrew's still all het up about John Mason cuttin' some of his timber."

"How did you figure that? I didn't hear Mr. Renfrew say anything about timber or Mr. Mason."

"Oh, it warn't hard," Manda said with a chuckle. "John Mason was over on Monday."

Rachel still didn't understand. "What's that got to do with Grandy?"

"John's told his side. Now Charlie will tell his. Then Jonathan will make a judgment. That's all there is to it," Manda explained.

"You mean Grandy's a judge?"

"Not exactly. Jonathan's a fair man. That's not easy to come by. Folks just naturally seek him out to help settle things peaceful-like."

"Oh," Rachel said, then, puzzled again, added, "But I thought Jason said Grandy was a real fighter with a terrible temper."

"He is a real fighter in a good cause and he does have a right fearful temper," Manda said. "Though he's learned to control it some. Back in his young days he was a real wild-cat, or so everyone tells me. Used to get into all kinds of mischief. But he outgrowed that. Outgrowin' that temper has taken a mite longer. Still he's a fair man and a natural born leader."

Manda's eyes glowed with a special pride that made Rachel proud of her grandfather, too.

"Has he ever lost his temper with you, Manda?"

"Many times."

"What do you do?" asked Rachel, wide-eyed.

"Lose mine right back at him." Manda laughed. "It always works, too. It makes Jonathan laugh when I get mad. He says I look like a little banty hen. He forgets to be angry then."

Rachel laughed too as she pictured a feisty little Manda hen standing up to an angry Grandy rooster.

"Reckon we do make quite a pair," Manda said with a smile. "Now let's get back to work. I'm sick of cabbage, too! This should be our last batch for a while. Sunday can't come too soon for me!"

"Me either," Rachel said, chopping vigorously.

Visitors might drop by during the week, but Sunday was a day for whole families to go visiting. Sometimes a whole wagonload of people came by for a visit. Sometimes Grandy got out the buckboard and they went off for a ride or a visit. Rachel often wondered how she could have thought there were no people in the valley.

One visitor had not been around much all summer— Mary Ann. Only once had she come to a family gathering and then she had avoided Rachel. That suited Rachel just fine. She had no wish to talk with Mary Ann while the memory of that awful night on the mountain still gave her nightmares.

Sunday morning dawned clear and hot. Once again it was the Carders' turn to host the circuit rider. From the size of the crowd it looked as if everyone in two counties had decided to attend the services.

After the first preaching Martha and Manda were sitting on the front porch waiting for everyone to finish eating.

46

"Mary Ann's courtin' a little with Clem Turner from down Walnut Grove," Martha announced proudly.

"That Jesse Turner's youngest boy?" Manda asked, trying to place Clem in her mind.

"That's right. Clem's the only one home now. The two girls married and left home two, three years ago. And, Everett, that's the oldest boy, he left home soon as he was sixteen. Nobody ever did hear anymore from him. Said he wuz going west. Just Clem and Jesse running that whole Turner place now."

"Reckon Jesse's right anxious to have Clem git married and settle down then," Manda surmised.

"Well, Jesse's no spring chicken. It would ease his mind some, I reckon. That's a pretty good size place to run with only two men." Martha glanced fondly over at Mary Ann. "Mary Ann's been sweet on Clem for quite a spell. She likes the Turner place, too, being closer to town and all. Seems like he just started noticin' her this summer."

Martha looked at Mary Ann who was taking care of the babies while the mothers ate dinner.

"I 'spect she's ready to leave the nest. Mary Ann always has known just what she wanted. Lordy, I sure am goin' to miss her. No other woman in the house. You're lucky to have Rachel to keep you company." Martha sighed.

"More than lucky, Martha, blessed," Manda said.

"Her turn will come soon enough," Martha allowed.

Rachel and Jason had heard every word said by Aunt Martha and Manda. They hadn't been eavesdropping. It was purely accidental. They had been sitting around the corner of the porch eating their dinner in the shade of the house. Of course, neither of them tried not to hear. They were, in fact, very quiet during the whole conversation.

After Manda and Aunt Martha left, Jason stood up

and dusted off his britches. "That was a good dinner. Guess it will hold me till supper. 'Specially after that good dessert!"

"What dessert, Jason? You haven't even had dessert yet." Rachel said, puzzled.

"The sweet news that Mary Ann's caught her a fellow, Miss Wide-Eyes!"

"Oh, Jason! You're being mean. And my eyes are not wide!" Rachel laughed at Jason's foolish grin.

"I'm not being mean, Rachel. I'm glad Mary Ann's got what she wants. If she wants Clem that's fine with me. He's a good ten years older'n her and ugly as a mud fence."

Rachel sobered. "That doesn't matter, Jason, if she loves him."

"Well, I'd say she's more in love with the Turner place than she is with Clem," Jason retorted. " 'Course girls are supposed to get married and leave home. Come on, let's get some pie before the preacher eats it all. He's had six pieces already."

Rachel shook her head at Jason's antics and moved off at a more sedate pace to get her own dessert. She chose a big piece of the blueberry cobbler, topped it with thick cream, and, since Jason was off cavorting with some boys, she went back to find a piece of shade for herself. She wanted to be alone to think about what Jason had said about getting married.

Rachel chose a corner on the side of the cabin near the open shutters of the parlor. She had barely begun eating her pie when voices floated out the window interrupting her thoughts.

"Where's your cousin, Mary Ann? She too good to lend a hand with the babies?"

"I don't expect she knows much about babies," Mary Ann replied. "Or anything else for that matter."

"Maybe she got lost," another voice said, giggling.

"Most likely," Mary Ann agreed smugly.

"You two are being mean! You just might git lost yourselves if you was in a big city for the first time."

"Aw, Josie, we ain't bein' mean. It's the God's truth. At least if I was lost I could tell uphill from downhill and know which direction to take! I think Miss Rachel is a pound short, even if she does wear them fancy clothes."

"Ah, ha! Lizzy's just jealous of her new clothes!"

"Am not!"

"Are, too!"

"Sh-h-h! We'll never get these babes to sleep, if you keep yellin'," Mary Ann hissed.

"Don't you shush me, Mary Ann Carder! You're no better than Lizzy. You're practically green with jealousy."

"Me? What could I be jealous over? A stray dog taken in? A crybaby who cain't find her way to the outhouse? A prissy show-off? A dumb outlander?"

" 'Pears to me like your nose is out o' joint! Maybe she don't know lots o' things, but I hear tell she's learned to ride as good as your Grandy Carder. And I just heard Miz Manda tell Ma that Rachel was a big help!"

"Well, I hope Miz Manda don't get to dependin' on all that help," Mary Ann said bitingly. " 'Cause most likely the first man that comes along, Miss Rachel'll run off with and marry. She's just trash, like her no-good mama!"

Rachel didn't wait to hear anymore. She was so angry she felt ready to explode. Her first impulse was to run into the house and yank Mary Ann's hair out by the roots and smash her teeth in. Only the thought of all the ruckus it would make stopped her. Instead, she walked stiffly into the woods at the side of the house.

Once out of sight of the cabin, Rachel vented her hurt

and anger on an innocent oak. She kicked and pounded on it until she felt somewhat better. At least she wasn't going to explode where everyone could see her.

Why had Mary Ann said those things?

What had she ever done to Mary Ann to make her call her names like stray dog, crybaby, or prissy show-off?

Those names stung like pinpricks. But calling her mother "trash" was like a sword in her heart.

Memories of her mother tumbled through her mind. Her mother with her wide, generous mouth, laughing and telling her stories when she'd been sick with chicken pox. The little frown that puckered between her eyebrows when she was upset or when Rachel had been naughty. The love and pride on her mother's face as she sat sewing Rachel's Easter dress—the very white dress she had on right now. It was the last thing her mother had made for her.

Tears sprang into Rachel's eyes as she remembered the countless hours her mother had spent doing things for her —not only feeding her and clothing her, but seeing that she always minded her manners, went to church and to school no matter what town they happened to be in—all of the little things she'd taken for granted so often. A person like that wasn't trash! And somebody saying it didn't make it so. Especially if that somebody was a fool like Mary Ann!

Somewhat calmer, Rachel started back to the meeting, hoping she hadn't been missed. Later, when she could get Mary Ann alone, she'd settle her score with her.

The opportunity came just as Rachel came out of the woods. Mary Ann was sashaying smugly up the path to the privy. Anger welled up inside Rachel again and spilled over. Quickly she crossed over and blocked Mary Ann's way. They were well out of view of the rest of the gathering.

50

"Oh, there you are. Manda was looking for you," Mary Ann said innocently.

"She can wait," Rachel replied tersely. "I want to talk to you."

Mary Ann looked into Rachel's icy blue eyes and backed up a step. "What do you want? Hurry up, I have to go," she said, trying to move around Rachel.

Rachel gripped her shoulders in a tight, punishing grip. "You'll stay here until I'm finished with you!"

"Ow! You're hurting me. Let go!" Mary Ann whined, trying to twist free.

"Not until I've had my say. You had your turn in the parlor a while ago."

"I—I didn't—"

"Don't deny it, Mary Ann! You're a liar."

"Am not! I only spoke the truth. If it hurts your feelings, too bad," Mary Ann ventured, trying to look righteous.

It was too much for Rachel. She was filled with a murderous rage. Letting go of Mary Ann's arms, she grabbed Mary Ann's throat in both hands and squeezed.

"I don't care what you think about me. It doesn't matter. But don't you ever—I mean *ever*—call my mother trash again!" With every word Rachel squeezed harder. She wanted to hurt Mary Ann. Stop her foul mouth forever . . . punish her. . . .

"S-stop. Stop. . . ." Mary Ann croaked, her fingers tearing at Rachel's hands.

"Promise you'll never say anything bad about my mother ever again."

"I—I—prom—ise—" Mary Ann gasped, sagging to the ground.

Her fall broke Rachel's grip. It also snapped the angry

51

miasma that clouded her mind. She looked down at Mary Ann's crumpled form and was appalled at what she had done. Without a word, she turned and hurried away before Mary Ann could see her tears of shame.

7

What's the matter with me? What am I going to do?

The murderous rage she had felt toward Mary Ann had shaken her deeply. Rachel needed some time alone to think.

After a restless night, she rose at first light, donned her riding clothes, penned a note to Manda, and slipped quietly downstairs. She left the note on a table by the stove, grabbed a few cold biscuits, and went down to the meadow to catch Bright Star.

"We'll stick to the trail," she told Star. "That way we won't get lost."

The dense woods and mountains still frightened Rachel. For the three months she had been at Carder's Cove she had scarcely gone off Carder land. Mostly it had been visits to Uncle Lem's or Roscoe's places. Those trails she avoided now.

Star seemed to think it was an adventure to be out of the meadow on such a fine morning.

Rachel's heart was not so light.

What on earth had come over her yesterday? For a few

moments she had wanted to kill Mary Ann! All over a few spiteful words that she knew weren't true. Oh, she knew she had a temper. She'd had temper tantrums before. But nothing like this. What was the matter with her?

Bright Star jogged along with Rachel so lost in thoughts that she was unmindful of their direction. She couldn't find any answers no matter how hard she tried. All she knew was that there was something mean lurking inside of her. And that she mustn't ever let it out again! If she didn't understand what had happened, how could she explain her actions to Grandy and Manda? What kind of story would Mary Ann tell? Should she have told Manda about it last night instead of rushing off to bed pleading a headache? Maybe the whole family would disown her and ship her back to Nashville or somewhere. Could she honestly say it would never happen again? She realized she wasn't the least bit sorry that she'd confronted Mary Ann about her vicious lies. She was only sorry she'd tried to throttle her!

The sun was beating down full upon Rachel and she was sweating. She had ridden out of the deep woods and was on the road to the Watauga Settlement.

"We've gone far enough, Star," Rachel said, turning Star back the way they had come. "I'm hot and thirsty. I bet you are, too. We'll find a creek and cool off."

It was easier said than done. Rachel had to ride almost an hour before she came to a creek that wasn't too far off the trail. Only after turning down a well-worn side trail did she hear the welcome burble and splash of running water.

Rachel dismounted and let Star drink and graze while she cooled her face and her thirst in the cool, clear water.

Munching her cold biscuit, Rachel sat on the grassy bank of the stream.

Yellow and black butterflies flitted gracefully from the

black-eyed Susans to the yellow-centered daisies. A blue jay noisily scolded a squirrel as it ran across a nearby limb. A sudden puff of breeze flipped Rachel's hair from her face, cooling her.

It's strange, she mused, I don't feel like a stray. I feel like I belong here. Like part of the family. Manda has made me feel welcome and useful. So has Grandy. Everyone, except Mary Ann, has been kind and made me feel I belong. Why does Mary Ann hate me? Is she jealous, like Josie Hawkins said? What of? She has both of her parents, a whole bunch of kinfolk and even a sweetheart. Why should she be jealous of me?

As for being a crybaby, well, yes, I did cry when I was lost. No denying that. I wonder if Jason and Grandy told everyone that I was still afraid of these mountains? Maybe, but I doubt it.

Rachel looked down at her clothes and her hands, now rough and tan, and smiled. By no stretch of her imagination could she think of herself as prissy. Yes, her clothes were fancier than most folks', but only because that was all she had. She would rather have clothes like Mary Ann's. They would be much more practical and comfortable.

And, if being a show-off meant trying to do her best, then she was guilty. She wanted to learn to ride as well as Grandy and to sew, cook, and keep house as well as Manda. If that was wrong, so be it. She wasn't going to change to suit Mary Ann!

A whiff of pungent smoke assailed Rachel's nose and interrupted her thoughts.

Bright Star smelled it, too, and snorted her displeasure.

"Come on, Star. Let's go see who's making such an awful stink," Rachel said.

Following her nose, Rachel came to a clearing and

recognized Granny Sharp's cabin. One of the few times she'd been off Carder land had been to a church service at Granny Sharp's.

"Hullo, Cabin!" Rachel called, remembering her mountain manners.

Granny Sharp's pert form appeared from the back of the cabin.

"Howdy, Rachel. Anybody sick up your way?"

"No, ma'am. I was just out for a ride and I smelled your smoke."

"Smells awful, don't it?" Granny Sharp chuckled. "Well, get down and visit a spell if you can stand it. Juner and me are out back."

Rachel dismounted, tied Star to the hitching post, and followed Granny Sharp.

Juner was stirring a huge black kettle over an open fire. Sweat trickled down his broad face, which broke into a wide grin at the sight of Rachel.

"Howdy, Miss Rachel. You cum to stir the pot? Hit smells awful but hit'll cure what ails you."

"Will it cure a terrible temper?" Rachel blurted. The words slipped out before she could stop them.

"I don't rightly know," Juner answered, puzzled.

Granny Sharp cocked her head on one side and peered at Rachel. "This mixture's good for coughs, colds, rheumatiz, and an assortment of other ills, but I don't know of a cure for a bad temper. Wish I did. I could make fame and fortune with it in these hills."

"I was only teasing," Rachel said quickly.

Granny Sharp smiled at her and said no more for the moment.

Juner let Rachel stir the pot while he went for a cool dipper of water and brought up some logs.

Rachel was so short she had to stand on a chunk of firewood to get a good hold on the stir-stick.

Granny Sharp added dried leaves and powders to the boiling pot. She kept her workers entertained with stories of the curing powers of her special brew. Finally satisfied with her concoction, she had Juner bank the fire to allow "aging" time.

"Come have a bite o' lunch with us now. You've earned it," she invited.

The cold buttermilk, brown beans, and corn pone tasted heavenly to Rachel. She watched in silent amazement as Juner downed a whole pone, four helpings of beans, and four mugs of buttermilk.

"Reckon that'll hold me till supper," he said, wiping his mouth on his sleeve.

"Juner has a healthy appetite. He works hard and eats hard," Granny Sharp explained. "Food don't even have to be good just so there's lots of it."

"It was mighty good," Rachel said. "Wish I'd had room for more of it. But I'd bust if I ate another bean. Besides, I'd better get going. Manda will be needing me for chores, I guess."

Granny Sharp walked out to the hitching post with Rachel.

" 'Pears to me like you are a mite troubled," she said as Rachel mounted.

Rachel nodded.

"Look, honey. You come by that temper honest. Your granddaddy has a notable temper. Manda has a temper. And your ma had one, too. So you come by it naturally. It's what you do with it that counts. A man or a woman without a sense of righteous anger ain't worth a lick o' salt. But a mean-minded man or woman is a trial and tribulation to everyone. I don't think you are mean-minded. You just have to work on keepin' that temper in line. Save it for when you need it. There'll be times when you need it, too, never fear. It's a lifetime job, I reckon, but you can do it if you try."

"Thanks, Granny Sharp. I sure am going to try."

"You keep to the mountain ways and you'll be just fine, Rachel. It's all still new to you, but it's what works for us. And you're one of us now."

"I'll try," Rachel promised. "Thanks again."

"Say howdy to Jonathan and Manda for me. You come again."

"I will. 'Bye, Juner," Rachel called as she rode out.

Juner waved vigorously. He liked Rachel.

Rachel felt a little better as she rode home. If Granny Sharp thought she could control her temper then, by cracky, she could. What was done was done. She'd try to make amends for that. But from now on she'd keep a tight rein on that Carder temper she'd come by so honestly.

Following the mountain ways was another matter. The more she thought about having to get married sometime and leave Grandy and Manda, the more upset she became.

Why was it considered necessary by mountain people? Who would she choose? Or who would choose her? Where would they live? How soon did she have to go?

"Where in thunderation have you been, Rachel?" Grandy bellowed at Rachel as she rode into the stable yard.

"Just out riding, Grandy. I told you I'd be gone a while. I had some thinking to do." Rachel knew Grandy wasn't really angry, just concerned. "I'm sorry if I worried you." Rachel unsaddled Bright Star and started to rub her down.

"Didn't worry *me* that you missed your breakfast and noon meal. But Manda was clucking like a wet hen. Here,

I'll do that," Grandy said. "You go on up to the house and smooth her ruffled feathers."

Rachel ran toward the house calling, "I'm home, Manda."

Manda came out the back door at the sound of Rachel's first words.

"Sake's alive, Rachel. I hope you don't do this often. Grandy was going out to look for you. You've been gone since before sunup."

"I left you a note on the table, Manda, honest! I just wanted to be alone for a while and think."

"Wind must have blown it off, honey. There was no note—and no Rachel. Never mind, wash up and come and eat. I kept some food warm for you."

Rachel was crawling around on the floor. "I see it, Manda. I see it! Over there, under the stove—my note."

Manda bent down and peered under the stove. Sure enough, there was a slip of white paper tucked in one corner. Manda retrieved it. "Now, whilst you wash up, Miss Rachel, I'll read this hidden treasure."

Rachel, having washed up, sat down to eat. She only picked at her food though.

"Thought you'd be hungry as a bear," Manda said, sitting down beside Rachel.

"Oh, I took some biscuits for breakfast. And, about noontime, I met Granny Sharp and Juner. They shared some food with me."

"Want to tell me what's eatin' on you then?"

Rachel hesitated only a moment, then burst out. "I don't want to leave here! I love this place and you and Grandy!"

"Leave? Who said you had to leave here?"

"Girls here all get married and have to leave home,

don't they? It isn't fair! Boys get to stay on their own place. Girls have to go! I'm just as old as Mary Ann. Soon I'll have to go, too. And, I don't want to!" By now Rachel was sobbing as if her heart would break.

Grandy came into the kitchen. "What's wrong? Is she hurt? Rachel. . . ."

"Rachel doesn't want to get married," Manda said calmly.

"Doesn't want to get married?" Grandy shouted. Then, realizing what he had said, asked, "Why?"

"She doesn't want to leave here—and us."

"Who said she had to leave?"

"Girls are supposed to get married and go off with their husbands. Mary Ann is, you know."

"O-oh, I see," said Grandy gravely. "She got anybody in mind she don't want to marry?"

"Nobody in particular, I reckon."

"Now, see here, Miss Rachel! You just stop your cater-wauling and listen to me." Grandy's blue eyes flashed with humor and exasperation. "You don't have to leave here or us until you've a mind to. This is your home for as long as you want it to be. Never you mind what everyone else does! You hear me, Rachel?"

"Y-yes, sir." Rachel gulped. Though Grandy's voice was loud and gruff, somehow it comforted Rachel and gave her courage to confess her other problems.

"I had a fight with Mary Ann yesterday," she blurted out.

Grandy and Manda exchanged glances.

"Was it over the trick she played on you?" Manda asked.

"No."

"What was it then?"

"Something she said that wasn't true," Rachel answered cautiously. She suddenly knew she couldn't tell them the awful thing that Mary Ann had said about their daughter.

"Don't worry on it," Grandy advised with a chuckle. "Young'uns are always fightin'."

"I tried to kill her," Rachel whispered.

"What?"

"I don't know what came over me. One minute I was just shaking her and the next thing I knew I was choking her! I was so mad I really wanted to kill her."

"When was this?" Manda asked.

"After lunch. The preacher was on his second sermon."

"I saw Mary Ann after that. She looked all right to me," Manda said.

"I don't think she was bad hurt. She fell down before I finished," Rachel explained. "What bothers me is that I got so mad that I wanted to kill her."

Once again it was Grandy who tried to comfort Rachel. He sat down beside her and took her hand in his large bony ones.

"Rachel, you see that kettle over yonder on the stove?"

Rachel nodded, stealing a glance at the kettle and lowering her eyes once more. She just could not look squarely at Grandy or Manda. She couldn't face their disappointment.

"When it gets hot enough, it'll boil," Grandy continued. "Folks are a lot like kettles. Now some kettles take a big ole hickory fire to get 'em boilin'. Other kettles will boil with just a tiny, well-placed kindlin' fire under 'em. It's good to know what kind o' kettle you are. Now you know. And no real harm done. So from now on, when you start to boil over, you just put yourself on the back burner till you simmer down a mite. Believe me, it works. I know, 'cause I'm one o' those fast kettles myself."

"You mean you aren't mad at me? Or ashamed of me?" Rachel asked, looking into Grandy's eyes for the first time.

" 'Pears to me like you learned your lesson," Grandy said softly. "I'd say you and Mary Ann are about even."

"Even?"

"Well, now, she tried to do you harm and you tried to do her harm. Mayhap both o' you learned something."

"I hope so," Manda said tartly. "I don't hold with kin against kin."

"I learned something," Rachel said solemnly. "I'll keep watch on this temper from now on."

"Good," Grandy said, rising from his chair. "Enough of these long faces now! We'd best be gettin' back to work if we're going to be gone for a few days."

"Gone where?" Rachel asked.

"Down to the Settlement. Me and the boys are taking a few horses down to the sales. Reckon you'd feel up to comin' along?"

Rachel's eyes sparkled with delight. "Oh, could I go, Manda? Jason says the horse sales are loads of fun."

"I reckon I could manage a day or so without you two underfoot," Manda said with a smile. "Probably be the most rest I've had in years."

"Why don't you come with us?"

"My bones are too old to jog around on horseback. But you can fetch me some supplies from Tipton's store, Rachel. And you'd best pick out some dress material. You're growin' right out o' your clothes."

Rachel laughed. "I don't think I could ride in one of my dresses."

"Probably not," Manda agreed. "Your clothes are not suitable for a young woman on horseback. I been thinking on this for some time now. What you need is a ridin' skirt. I made one for your mama years ago. I think I stored it somewheres. With a little alterin', you could wear it."

"Where is it? Let's fix it now!"

"Chores first, young lady! I'll fix it tonight onct I've dug it out," Manda promised.

"Yes, ma'am," Rachel said happily. "What do you want me to do?"

"The beans need pickin'. Then we can string some for dryin'."

Rachel grabbed a dishpan and hurried out to the garden. Her heart felt light as a feather. Grandy and Manda really did love her and want her to stay! Even with her bad temper they loved her.

"She's a good little lass," Manda said with a smile.

"Aye, that she is," agreed Grandy.

Unwittingly, Grandy fanned the dying embers of Mary Ann's jealousy into a smoldering, vengeful resentment.

First he allowed Rachel to ride Bright Star into the Settlement instead of making her ride in the wagon with Mary Ann and the other womenfolk.

Hugh Tipton added coals to the fire by giving Rachel a sweeping bow. "Is this the same girl who bounced out of here on old Bess? I think not! This beautiful horsewoman is someone else. You've thrown a ringer at me, Jonathan, you ole horsetrader!"

Grandy chuckled with pride. "It's the same lass, Hugh. What did you expect? She's my granddaughter."

Rachel flushed with pleasure.

Mary Ann reddened with anger, but as Lem pulled the wagon away from the store, she stretched her lips into a smile and called, "I'll see you later, Rachel."

Martha, too, was aware of the special attention being given to Rachel, while no one paid any particular notice to her daughter. "You change into something presentable before you come out meeting folks, Rachel," she said loudly. "You smell horsy!"

"I will," Rachel promised, flushing.

Later, Grandy really threw the fat into the fire. He bought six yards of Hugh's best blue-flowered cloth for Rachel.

It was the very material Mary Ann coveted for herself. Her pa told her she couldn't have it because it was too pricy.

Rachel was unaware of any change in Mary Ann, either for better or worse. She stuck close to Jason and Grandy, avoiding Mary Ann and Aunt Martha, for the whole delightful two days.

The only thing that marred the trip for Rachel was the frightening talk of war that cropped up at the Tiptons' supper table.

Mrs. Tipton was a large-boned, handsome woman with kind gray eyes and a no-nonsense manner.

"Supper is on the table. Find your places, gentlemen, and let's eat before everything gets cold," she told the assorted group of men gathered in her parlor. "Rachel, it looks like you and me are the only ladies, so you sit by me so we can talk."

The food set forth was simple, plentiful, and delicious. The men attacked it with gusto. Nothing much was said except the "please-pass-me's" until appetites were satisfied. Then the talk centered on politics.

The Watauga Settlement might be in the backwoods, but the people were keenly interested in what was going on in the rest of the nation. Most of their forefathers had fought for independence less than a hundred years ago. Now it seemed that this nation so newly formed was having problems.

Mrs. Tipton and Rachel listened in silence as the talk ebbed and flowed around them.

"Them northerners in Congress are gettin' pretty high-handed. The South won't stand still for that kind of treatment."

"Mr. Lincoln is a sensible man. He can cool off those hotheads."

"Don't think one man can do much, though I voted for Abe myself."

"Ira's right. We fought the British for our independence. I, for one, don't take kindly to losing it again to some know-it-all northern Congressmen."

"Seems to me like a little give and take on both sides would work wonders," Grandy said mildly.

"Yep. They want to give orders and us to take 'em! Raise your cotton—sell it cheap—pay high tariffs on all the goods we send you—slavery's wrong—free the slaves—" The man paused for breath. His face was flushed and angry.

"Now, John, you don't own any slaves, do you? Or raise any cotton, either," Hugh said in a half-joking manner.

"No, I don't! But if I did, I'd want the right to decide for myself what to do with my own. So would any man here!" John thundered, hitting his fist on the table.

"Now that's part of the trouble," Grandy's voice cut in. "Everybody gets hot under the collar and that's the end of reason. Pretty soon you have two sides yellin' at each other and nobody listenin'."

A murmur of assent went around the room, except for the flush-faced man, John. He refused to be mollified. "It just might work out better if we had two countries, like some are sayin'. North and South don't think alike."

Grandy's eyes flashed. "Think now, man! We are the *United* States of America. We must learn to settle our differences. We can't survive divided. My father fought for this nation—one nation—just as yours did. We need the North and they need us."

Jonathan Carder was a hard man to disagree with, especially when he was angry. No one did, outloud.

"I hope those Yankees know that, Jonathan," Hugh said, rising. "If they keep pushing, I'm afraid some of the southern states will exercise their right to pull out of the Union."

There were more determined nods than Jonathan liked to see. He, too, rose and said thoughtfully, "I hope so, too, because if they don't it will mean war."

"War?" Rachel exclaimed in spite of herself. "Who are we going to fight, Grandy?"

All eyes turned toward Rachel.

"That's a good question, Rachel. You men best be keepin' that question and the answers in mind before you go off half-cocked."

On that sobering note everyone filed out of the room.

Mulling over these events kept Rachel awake a long time.

October's bright blue skies heralded an autumn that would remain etched in Rachel's memory. The trees were a riot of colors. Maples—red, gold, and orange. Oak—red and rust. Poplars—yellow and silver. Chestnuts, hickory, locusts, and sycamores provided the shades in between. The whole spectrum was so bright it almost hurt her eyes.

Each morning when the sun burned away the mists, it was like the curtain going up on a stage. The air was crisp and cool with a fragrant tang to it. The day would gradually get warm, almost summery. The bees would come out and make a last stab at the goldenrods and black-eyed Susans.

Squirrels chattered and scurried endlessly. Large flights of birds often darkened the sky on their way to winter homes. Evenings were cooler now with a nip of frost in the air. Even the stars looked bigger and brighter. The moon, not to be outdone, was a soft, mellow orange ball sailing majestically along the starry way.

"It's so beautiful, I don't want it to ever end."

"Indian summer is my favorite time of year, too," Manda said. "Seems like I always have so much to do gettin' ready for winter, I don't get enough time to enjoy it all."

"I guess I must've missed most of the other falls. I don't ever remember anything like this in Nashville," Rachel mused. "Maybe it was because I was in school. When does school start here, Manda?"

"Usually about the second week of October. Most of the harvestin' is done by then. Reckon that would be this coming Monday. It's been a while since I had anyone going off to school, Rachel." Manda laughed. "What grade did you finish last year?"

"Eighth. I'd be in the Upper Form this year at Nashville."

Manda's face looked troubled. "Our school only goes through grade eight, Rachel. If a young'un's real bright and wants to go on, he goes into town to boarding school."

Rachel clearly was stunned. She had liked school and assumed she would be going whenever school started.

Manda saw Rachel's confusion and tried to explain the situation. "It's not that we don't hold with education, Rachel. We do. But there's not too many families out here. Most families need every pair of hands available to help run their places. So most folks send their young'uns as soon as they can spare 'em from the farm in October—till they're needed again in the spring—about April. They learn to read, write, and figure pretty well. We're lucky here at Carder's Cove. Miz Julie took over two years ago when her husband died and she teaches seventh and eighth graders Latin, geography, and history besides the regular schoolwork."

"Does Jason go to school?"

"He's in eighth grade this year. Miz Julie says he's smart, but he doesn't work very hard at his studies."

"Mary Ann? Does she go to school?"

"She finished last year. Good thing, I reckon! She won't have her mind on schoolwork this year. Martha says they'll probably announce the wedding at Sunday's meeting. Most likely be in early spring."

"That's nice. I hope they'll be happy," Rachel said absently.

"Don't you fret. You'll have a peck o' learning to do this winter even if it doesn't come from books," Manda said.

Rachel nodded glumly. She'd really counted on going to school and making some friends.

The announcement of Mary Ann's wedding brought Rachel problems. The good news triggered a flurry of social activity. First there were the "hope chest" parties. Women would gather at different homes to help make things to fill Mary Ann's hope chest. These usually took place on Saturday and lasted all day.

Mary Ann loved it. She was the center of attention and she gathered many lovely and useful things to start her off in her new role.

These parties were pure torture for Rachel. She didn't like sewing, quilting, or weaving in the first place. She'd rather be doing anything other than sitting and sewing all day.

Mary Ann never lost an opportunity to point out

Rachel's discomfort or her mistakes—always with put-on kindness, of course.

"My goodness, you're restless, Rachel. I reckon you'd rather be out riding Star. Of course, it's a little cold for me, but I'm not very hardy."

"Oh, Rachel, you've mismatched a piece! Never mind, I'll fix it. You've pricked your finger and it might bleed on the quilt."

"Not that way, Rachel. Watch Janey. See what tiny stitches she makes? She's the best seamstress I know."

Rachel bore all the jibes in silence. Mary Ann had a knack of making it impossible for her to answer without seeming churlish.

The other women were never unkind, but Mary Ann did create an image of Rachel as clumsy and unwomanly.

Manda saw what was happening but she couldn't help. Any intervention on her part would have made matters worse.

One day as they were driving home from a quilting party, Rachel exploded. "Why does she do this to me? I've never done one single solitary thing to her! Except try to choke her. I wish I'd finished the job now!"

Rachel's face was a dusky red as she whipped the team into a dangerously fast pace.

"Whoa down, Rachel! Take it a mite easier on the horses. You'll overturn us both and that won't help," Manda said, clinging to the wagon seat with both hands.

Rachel slowed the team.

"That's better," Manda said, relaxing her grip. "You've done me real proud up to now, Rachel. You've held on to that temper. I know Mary Ann's been pokin' you in a sensitive spot. And I know why. Till you come along Mary Ann was the queen bee—the only girl in the family. All o' us spoiled her. It's not surprisin' that she don't like sharin' her hive with you, is it?"

"No, I figured that. But I haven't taken anything away from her! She has just what she had when I came. Even more. Now she has Clem!"

"But not all the attention. You live with us, ride like you was born to it, and everyone knows you're here. It don't escape Mary Ann's notice! So, the worse she makes you look the better she looks accordin' to her way of thinkin'. She's purty sharp. Or thinks she is."

"Oh, she is," Rachel said grimly. "The more she goes on about my mistakes, the more I make. And little Miss Maple Syrup knows it!"

Manda chuckled. "Don't she though! But, believe it or not, you're winnin', if you don't blow up on her."

"How do you figure that?"

"She'll overplay her hand. Folks will catch on. Same as me. Then they'll remember your patience and not your temper."

"All right, Manda. I'll try to keep my mouth shut. Even if my tongue gets four inches shorter!"

Manda smiled, but said seriously, "I reckon Mary Ann's only part of your problem. She's found her place. She knows what she wants. I don't think you've found yours yet. You're still lookin' and learnin'. When you find it, you'll be satisfied in your soul. Just wait. You'll see."

Manda's words gave Rachel comfort and something to hold onto the next time Mary Ann tried to kill her with kindness.

The "sociables" posed a different problem than the "hope chest" gatherings.

During the fall and winter months different families would have work parties for picking apples, making apple

71

butter, corn husking, or hog killing and sausage making. After the work was finished there would be a sociable, with music and games for the young folks, all under the watchful eyes of their elders. The choosing and courting of future mates were done at these events.

Rachel loved the work parties. About the sociables she had mixed feelings. She liked the music, dancing, and games, but she hated feeling like a filly in an auction ring. She was filled with a numbing dread each time a party began. What if no one chose her to dance or play? Would she have to sit on the sidelines like some of the other women with a smile frozen on her face? What if she were chosen? Did that mean she would have to let some man court her, or even marry one she hardly knew?

The eligible men came in all ages, sizes, and shapes. The younger men puzzled her. She had expected them to be like Jason, laughing, talking, and full of fun. They weren't. They were more like her other cousins, shy, silent, and tentative. She couldn't get to know any of them. The older men were more outgoing and forceful. But they often put her off with their self-assurance and sometimes sly jokes.

Having no one her own age to talk with about her feelings, Rachel suffered silently at each sociable. Mostly her fears were unfounded. She was picked often enough to dance or play a game and yet not by any one man.

The Ellis's corn husking party brought her feelings into the open.

A huge mound of unhusked corn was piled in the center of the barn. Somewhere hidden inside the mound was one red ear. Hopeful men young and old tore into the pile, shucking the ears clean and tossing them into a pile for the women to run through the shellers. The man who found the red ear got to kiss the girl of his choice.

The men worked quickly with much good-natured banter.

"Git ready, Mary Ann. I want me a nice buss 'fore you're done taken."

"I'll give you a bust, Sam Johnstone!"

"Pucker up, Sally! This is my lucky day!"

"I got a persimmon in my pocket, Henry, if you need a pucker!"

The teasing flew back and forth until John Cameron yelled, "I got it!"

Full-bearded, tobacco-chewing, two-hundred-pound John Cameron held up the ear of red corn. John was a thirty-five-year-old widower with four children. He made straight for Rachel.

Rachel wanted to run. Of all the older men, she liked John the least. He was loud, coarse, and always had a wad of tobacco tucked in his cheek. There was nowhere to go! The circle of women closed behind her.

John grabbed her and gave her her first kiss. It seemed to go on forever! His beard scratched and his breath stank.

Then John's hand pinched her bottom!

Rachel gasped. She swung her foot back and kicked him as hard as she could in the shins and, as he released her, she slapped his face.

The slap sounded like a pistol shot. All talk and laughter ceased.

Rachel glared at John. "Your red corn entitled you to a kiss. Nothing else. I'm not in the market for a husband, so you can keep your kisses and your hands to yourself! All of you!"

She pushed her way through the gawking women and left.

Word spread through the mountains like wildfire.

Some people laughed and said John got no more than he deserved.

Others frowned and said Rachel was uppity. After all, it was only a game.

Mary Ann went around apologizing for her cousin's unseemly behavior. Her joy was hard to hide. She'd evened the score. Now both the men and the women would shy away from this outlander. She'd branded herself as uppity and different. Even Manda and Grandy's good name wouldn't protect Miss Rachel now!

It mattered little to Mary Ann that she wouldn't be around to see the fruits of her labor. It was enough to know that Rachel would always be an outsider.

Manda said nothing about Rachel's tantrum. Instead she asked Grandy to set up her big wooden loom and her spinning wheels. She began teaching Rachel to spin flax on the "little" wheel and wool on the "big" wheel. Manda was famous for her high quality cloth, both linen and wool. She would pass this skill along to Rachel, she vowed.

Rachel couldn't seem to get the knack of feeding the new fiber to the spindle smoothly so there would be neither slubs nor weak places in the yarn.

"Takes practice," Manda said consolingly, when Rachel's yarn broke for the fifth time.

"I'll never learn to do it like you do," Rachel wailed. "I don't even want to try the loom. I'll ruin your cloth."

The wooden loom took up most of the room. Often Manda worked from sunup till sunset weaving the linsey-woolsey.

"Don't feel so, Rachel. Try again. I've been weavin' since I was knee high to a grasshopper. You cain't expect to master this in one winter. 'Sides, some folks have a natural talent for this kind of thing. Maybe you have and maybe you don't. Won't know till you try, now will you?"

"I guess not," Rachel replied with resignation. And she did try—with the same exasperating results. She had to restrain her impulse to give the little wheel a swift kick every time she passed by it.

Everyone seemed to have forgotten her outburst. At least, no one said anything. However, at the sociables she wasn't picked for a partner very often, except by her cousins and kin.

Rachel told herself it didn't matter. She was too old to dance and play silly games anyway. Much better to help the women pass out food.

But it did matter. Rachel had told them "hands-off" and the men took her at her word. And all winter Manda did try to teach her to spin and weave. As the winter rolled by, she felt more and more isolated.

At last, early spring brought the long awaited wedding festivities—three days and nights of merrymaking, climaxing in the Sunday wedding.

Every house for miles around was full. Twelve guests stayed in the cabin at Carder's Cove, plus a few hardy souls who camped in the barn. Most of them were relatives, both near and distant.

"Where did they all come from? How did they know?" Rachel asked Manda as they attacked another huge stack of dishes.

"The word passes." Manda laughed. "They're kin. The clan always gathers to celebrate or mourn with one of its own."

Mary Ann was a beautiful bride. Even Rachel thought so. However, she couldn't stifle a little sigh of relief as Clem and the new Mrs. Turner drove away on a wagon loaded with gifts.

At least she'll be miles away, thought Rachel, and busy being mistress of her own house.

Two days after the wedding a spring snowstorm buried the valley in a shroud of white.

At first Rachel enjoyed the peace and quiet. But as the days passed she grew more and more restless.

"Your first time's the worst," Manda allowed. "After a few years, a body gets accustomed to our chancy springs."

"I don't think I will!" Rachel said and went upstairs.

After the long winter, she felt as if the walls of the cabin were closing in on her—getting smaller every day. She was tired of her own company—of Manda and Grandy, too. Sometimes it felt as if the three of them were the only people left in this white wilderness. She longed for the sun, people, the sight of the mountains, birds—anything but the white blanket that covered everything.

When the thaw came Rachel was out of the cabin like a shot out of Grandy's rifle. She trampled happily through the slush to Jason's to see how they had fared.

Out riding one afternoon a week later, Rachel was surprised to see tiny green shoots of Manda's iris popping up along the creek bank.

"My goodness, it's spring!" Rachel gave Bright Star a nudge and went into the stable yard at a full gallop yelling —"Grandy! Manda! Spring's comin'. The iris are up!"

The iris weren't the only things that were up in the spring of 1861. Tempers flared in the halls of government in both North and South. The pot of trouble that had been brewing finally boiled over. Lincoln took office as President of a divided country in March. South Carolina fired on Union troops at Fort Sumter and the War between the States began in earnest.

Unaware of all this turmoil taking place outside the shelter of her misty mountains, Rachel was helping Manda with spring cleaning.

"A-a-choo!" Manda said, sneezing, as the feathers from the mattress she and Rachel carried out tickled her nose. "Heave this mattress over the line. Then we'll stop and catch our breath over a cup of tea."

As Manda and Rachel started back toward the cabin, they heard the thunder of a horse's hooves coming from the river road.

"Hallo-o-o, Cabin! Rachel! Manda!"

Recognizing the voice and the urgency in it, both of them ran for the front clearing.

Jason halted in a cloud of dust.

"What is it, Jason?"

"What's wrong?"

"*War*!" Jason shouted. "We're at *war*! Hugh Tipton just rode up to the lambing pens and told Grandy. I'm to go tell the others!" Jason wheeled Cherokee about and was ready to dash off when Manda grabbed the reins.

"Whoa, now, Jason. You just calm down a mite," she said sternly. "Who's at war? What's all this about?"

Jason clearly was impatient to be off on his important task, but Manda had a firm hold on Cherokee's head and was not to be put off.

"Hugh said South Carolina and some other states had pulled out of the Union. Didn't want to be a part of the United States. Lincoln says they can't do that. Anyways, some Rebel troops fired on Fort Sumter in South Carolina or something. It's war."

"Why is it war?" Rachel demanded. "What has South Carolina got to do with Tennessee?"

"Oh, cricky, Rachel! I haven't got time to tell you every detail. Please let me go, Manda. Grandy told me to ride to the head of the valley and up to Walnut Grove with the news." Cherokee was prancing about, sensing the excitement in the air, and Manda was having a hard time holding his head.

Manda released Cherokee and called at Jason's retreating back, "Be careful, Jason. Get your wits together before you go off like. . . ." Jason was out of earshot before she could finish.

Manda shook her head. "Men! There's nothing they like quite as much as a good fight!"

Rachel felt a cold shudder creep over her.

"I don't like fighting," she declared.

"Most women don't," Manda said as she headed back inside. "Probably wouldn't have wars if women ran things. But we don't."

Rachel followed slowly after Manda. "Will war come here? To our mountains? What's it all about, Manda? I don't understand this at all."

"Don't fret so, Rachel. Jonathan will explain it all to us when he gets in. I 'spect Jason was just stretchin' the truth a mite. After all, it is spring!" Manda said comfortingly.

But Jonathan couldn't explain it all to them when he came in because he didn't understand all of it himself.

"Some of the southern states have pulled out of the Union. They say it's their right. They've formed a new country—the Confederate States of America. The northern states say they can't do this. That it is not a right of each state to pull out if it wants."

"Has Tennessee resigned the Union?" Manda asked.

"Not yet. The legislators are meeting right now to decide," Grandy answered thoughtfully.

"Which way will they vote, Grandy?"

"I honestly don't know, Rachel. By geography and by custom and by interest we are a southern state. Still, most of the people around here believe in the Union. Their kin fought for it against the British. Most of our folks don't hold with slavery. We're an independent lot." Grandy shook his head in bewilderment. "I just don't know."

One day in late June, Hugh Tipton brought them the answer to their question. "I rode up to tell you, Jonathan. The legislators decided," he announced. "On June eighteenth, Tennessee seceded from the Union. We were the last southern state to withdraw. Will you pass the word along?"

Grandy nodded. "Aye, I will, Hugh."

Since Carder's Cove was tucked away in a corner of Tennessee almost inaccessible to armies of either side, the sounds of battle were unknown in their misty mountains. But despite the outward calm, the air in Carder's Cove was so unsettled that Rachel had ridden off by herself to think things out. She was frightened. Everything had changed. Yet nothing had changed. The mountains were the same— warm and protecting in the summer sun. The garden still needed weeding to protect the fast growing vegetables. The mares and young foals still romped in the pasture.

But people had changed. Not a shot had been fired in these mountains but people had changed. They "took sides," as Grandy had said. You couldn't tell who was on which side either. And you didn't dare ask. People in the same family might be on opposite sides. It had already happened in the Carder family. John and Matthew had gotten into a bad fight yesterday at the corral. It took both Uncle Lem and Uncle Roscoe to pull them apart before they killed each other. Then Uncle Roscoe and Uncle Lem almost got into it. Grandy sent everyone home to cool off. Everyone was to meet tonight at Carder's Cove for a family council.

"I hate it!" Rachel told Bright Star. "Why can't things be like they were? Why does everybody get mad at everybody? Who cares about some silly old war?"

Bright Star whinnied in sympathy.

"Oh, Star, I don't even know which side I'm for! North or South—either way somebody I love will get hurt. I don't want to take sides."

Hearing the anger and fright in Rachel's voice made Bright Star shift nervously and lay back her ears.

"Easy, Star, I'm not mad at you. It's this war amongst us that's got me riled!" Giving Bright Star a nudge, Rachel started reluctantly back to the house.

By six o'clock the whole Carder clan had gathered in the front parlor. It was an unusually quiet gathering. People were talking—but quietly. There was a feeling of tension underneath the subdued talk.

Grandy stood up and waited for the silence which came quickly. "Reckon we are all here. Might as well get started." He glanced down at Manda. "Manda and me was up most all last night talking over this war and how it bears on us Carders. We'd like to hear your ideas. That's why we called a family council. Might as well know how everybody feels and what he's goin' to do. You want to speak out first, Roscoe?"

"We've talked some at our place, too, Pa." Roscoe shifted his stance uneasily. "Reckon this ain't gonna blow over. Me and the boys feel the Union is more right than wrong!" He took a quick breath and spoke in a rush. "And if we have to, we'll fight to hold her together."

Matthew and Andrew could barely keep from cheering. Instead, they nodded their heads vigorously. Rose and Jason simply sat in silent agreement.

Lem jumped to his feet. "I've knowed you all of my life, Roscoe! You're my brother! I never heard you ever say anything so foolish before. You're a mountain man—a Tennessean, a southerner, by God! How can you say you'll fight for some outlander to come in here and tell you what to do? I don't know you!"

Grandy interrupted Lem's angry shouting. "Calm

down, Lem," he said with quiet authority. "Nobody here's deaf. Tell us what you plan to do."

"Do? John, Mark, and me are gonna do what any red-blooded mountain man would do. We're gonna defend our homes. We did it against the Indians and the British. We'll do it against the Yankees."

John and Mark were both on their feet with fire in their eyes.

"Right, Pa!"

"Won't take long to whip 'em either!"

"*Sit!*" Grandy thundered.

Like obedient hound dogs, they sat. But it was only a temporary truce out of respect for Jonathan Carder. The men were itching to trade blows instead of words.

"I've heard you out. Now, hear me out. You said just about what we expected, though how it's come about is a puzzlement to me, you and Lem being from the same family," Grandy said, looking at Roscoe. "This war is going to bring out much of this kind of difference. Each man will have to search his own heart and decide which side is right —if he can—and, then, act according to his own conscience." Grandy paused. Everyone waited expectantly.

"I've studied both sides. I don't think the Union is all right. And I don't think the Confederacy, as they call this new nation, is all right. There's some right and some wrong on both sides. I've examined my conscience and I can't decide. They're balanced. I'm too old to fight anyways. And it looks like I'll be giving a son and grandsons to each side— so I'm goin' to be neutral."

"Aw, Pa, you can't do that!"

"Nobody's gonna let you."

"I can and they will," Grandy stated with certainty. "This land is mine and I declare it neutral territory. I will allow no fighting on any part of it. What's more, Manda, Rachel, and I will give aid to any man who asks for it— northerner or southerner. As for the stock—Roscoe, you take half, Lem, the other half. Leave me with just Tam, a few brood mares, Bright Star, and old Moses. That fair enough, would you say?"

"Fair enough."

"More'n fair."

"One more thing—a man must do what he must. But under this roof, on this land, we are Carders, kinfolk— nothing else. You'll all be welcome here any time, if you observe that rule. Startin' right now."

A short silence followed. Then the tension broke and everyone started talking at once.

Manda and Aunt Rose went to the kitchen for coffee and cake for everyone.

Jason came over to sit by Rachel.

"How do you feel about this, Rachel?"

"It's queer you should ask, Jason. I was just sittin' here thinking—not one woman spoke up to say how she felt. No one even asked. Does Aunt Rose feel like Uncle Roscoe? Or Aunt Martha like Uncle Lem?"

Jason smiled at Rachel's questions. "Rachel, nobody asked 'cause they know the answer. A woman feels like her husband does!"

"How do you know? Did you ever ask?"

"Never had to. That's the mountain way."

"Well, it may be the mountain way, but it's not necessarily the right way!"

Jason frowned at her. "What's the matter, Rachel? Don't you agree with Grandy's way?"

"Oh, I agree. That's not the problem. He just didn't ask me if I agreed or not. He decided for me!"

"That's only because you are just a young'un. I bet he asked Manda her opinion. He wouldn't have dared not. She's little but she's feisty!"

"Who's little and feisty?" Manda asked as she came up with Jason's coffee and cake.

Jason blushed.

Rachel laughed at Jason's discomfort. Then she took pity on him. "Jason was just explaining a mountain woman's ways to me, Manda."

"Lordy, don't listen to him, Rachel. He hasn't had a whole lot of experience, I'll wager."

Jason blushed again and beat a hasty retreat to the men's side of the room.

The meeting ended soon afterward on a note of cautious friendliness.

"That's all settled then!" Grandy said as he blew out the lanterns in the parlor.

But, as Rachel went up to bed, she wondered if anything were settled, or ever would be again.

10

"I thought I heard something outside!" Rachel cocked her head and listened intently. In the process she dropped the yarn again.

" 'Tis only the wind," Manda said. "Here, try again. This time hold the yarn a mite tighter."

Sighing, Rachel picked up the yarn. Another winter had rolled around and she was dreading it. There weren't as many sociables now that so many men had gone to war. And with the coming of cold weather, out had come the loom and the spinning wheels. Manda was going to teach her if it killed them both.

The wind howled around the house like a banshee, spitting ice and snow. The November afternoon was already as dark as twilight. Manda had lit several lanterns.

A thunderous knock startled them both.

"Keep workin'. I'll see who 'tis," Manda said, stepping cautiously to the door. She opened the door a crack and then threw it wide. "Come in—come in. You must be frozen."

Two well-bundled figures—one large and one small—tumbled inside.

Granny Sharp and Juner proceeded to unwrap themselves from layers of clothing.

Rachel put another log on the fire as Manda hustled them over to it.

"What brings you two out on a day like this? Rachel, heat some water for tea. You all hungry?"

"Juner could eat," Juner said quickly.

"Juner can always eat," Granny Sharp replied, smiling. "I wouldn't say no to a cuppa tea though."

Rachel was only too glad to have an excuse to stop her weaving lesson. She ran to the pantry to get some nutcakes to go with their tea.

"We been over to the Renfrews for two days, treating William's chest pains," Granny Sharp explained.

"He like t' died," Juner added, "but Granny saved him."

"This time. Might not be so lucky next time. William's got a bad heart. Shouldn't be out huntin' alone, much less tryin' to tote that sixteen point buck by hisself."

"Warn't no one else to do it," Juner said practically.

"William isn't the only old man tryin' to do the work of two or three young ones," Manda said. "I worry some about Jonathan."

"Who's worrying about me?" Grandy asked. He had quietly slipped in the back way when he saw two strange horses outside. Now, he put up his rifle and joined Juner and Granny Sharp by the fire.

"I am," Manda replied.

"No need. Yon's the one you should be worryin' over. Granny, you look plum tuckered. You and Juner best stay the night. It's gettin' worse."

Granny Sharp sighed. "It wasn't so bad when we left this morning. I reckon these old bones could use a night's rest."

"What are you blathering about, Granny? You're just a spring chicken," Grandy teased.

"All I know is, I'm not as young as I was," Granny said. "It's hard enough to git out to see the sick but, even with Juner's help, I find gatherin' my herbs is a real chore. What frets me most is not havin' anyone to take over when I be gone."

Juner stopped eating and said with alarm, "Where you goin', Granny?"

"Nowhere any time soon, I hope." Granny reassured him.

"Truth to tell, we'd be hard up without you," Grandy said soberly. "No one else to do any doctorin' in these mountains for twenty or thirty miles."

"Could I help? I could help Juner collect herbs and I could write down some of Granny Sharp's remedies so that whoever takes over would know them. . . ." Rachel stopped when she saw Granny Sharp's brown eye twinkling with laughter.

"You know, Rachel, I was just hoping you'd offer to do that. I accept your offer."

Manda frowned, then laughed. "I'm thinking Miss Rachel just wants to get out of spinning and weaving," she said.

"That, too," Rachel admitted, laughing.

Granny Sharp kept her busy. At first she had only dried herbs. Then she learned how to make salves and ointments from the herbs and what each was for. During the long cold winter, she often spent a week at Granny Sharp's writing down the remedies for different ailments and watching Granny treat those who came to her for help. Gradually, Rachel began to help Granny treat patients.

"You've got the touch, Rachel!" Granny said one day as Rachel helped set a broken arm with splints and red clay.

"A touch of what, Granny?"

"The healing touch, honey. Them that's blessed with it make great doctors. Them that don't have it ain't worth a bag o' beans."

Rachel blushed. Pleased with the compliment, she worked even harder to increase her skill.

Before she knew it, the winter had passed. As her skills increased so did her satisfaction. The more she learned, the more she wanted to know. Her small hands, which couldn't manage a foot of yarn on the spinning wheel without a slub or a knot, moved deftly and soothingly as she stitched a wound or set a broken bone. In spite of her short temper she was always calm and understanding with people who were hurt or ill. Her impatience was usually reserved for herself when she didn't know how to do something.

"How did you ever learn so much, Granny Sharp?" Rachel asked.

A steady stream of people had kept them busy all day . . . two broken bones to set; a thigh gash to sew up, caused by an errant scythe; a colicky baby to soothe; a spider bite that had festered, and a man who'd been stung thirty times by hornets.

"Well, for one thing, I had a good teacher," Granny Sharp replied, settling back on her rocker with a cup of sassafras tea. "My papa was a doctor in England. When I was little he let me help in his surgery. In fact, despite his and Mama's best efforts, he couldn't keep me out. So he put me to work. Later, when we came to this country, I helped him, because there wasn't anyone else. Papa found lots of things different over here. Couldn't get help or medicines. Had no hospitals or surgeries in the wilderness either. But Papa made do. He was a naturalist. Believed that God put every animal and plant here for a purpose. So he made friends with an Indian medicine man and learned about plants over here. Fixed a room in our house for his surgery. And I was his help till I married Crockett Sharp. Even then I helped, twixt babies and house duties. When Papa died Crockett wanted to move further west. We got this far and homesteaded. Raised six young'uns here. Four girls and two boys. Guess doctorin' was in my blood though. I couldn't turn away a sick man, woman, or child. I had Papa's books and a little skill. I just kept on addin' to what I knew. John Quick-Fox has been a big help. He's a Cherokee medicine man, you know."

"I've heard him mentioned a time or two, but I've never seen him."

"He's gettin' up in years. Don't come by too often now. Anyways, that's how it's come about. After Crockett died I just kept on doctorin'. The young'uns married and moved on. Somehow I couldn't."

"I'm glad you didn't," Rachel said gratefully. "I'd never have had a chance to learn. I'm beholden to you."

"You're not beholden to me, Rachel! It's the other way around," Granny Sharp said sternly. "It's a good callin', but it does have drawbacks. You should know about them before you take on this work completely."

"What drawbacks? What could be better than helping folks who're sick?" Rachel asked in surprise.

Granny Sharp sighed and put down her teacup. Hitching her rocker up closer to Rachel, she said, "Doctorin' is sorta like gettin' bit by a snappin' turtle. It don't let go of a body till it's too late—if ever. You get a lot from doctorin', I'm not denyin' that. But doctorin' takes a lot from you, too."

"Like what? I know it takes time, but what else?"

Looking into Rachel's eager blue eyes, Granny Sharp said, "Time is important, Rachel. A body only has so much of it. Doctorin' can be special hard on a woman because it takes up time she's supposed to be using for her husband and children. You know how hard women in these hills have to work. Their work is important and necessary for a family to survive. So you're choosing a task that could keep you from doin' your duty as a wife and mother. Men don't take kindly to wives who put others before them."

"How did you manage?" Rachel shot back.

"Not very well sometimes. Crockett was a fair man. Better'n most. But we got into a few shoutin' matches ourselves when he felt neglected. Young'uns, too, at times. Billy Bob never did understand why I wouldn't move on to Texas with him and his family. I couldn't. Felt like I had to stay here and help folks who was countin' on me. Now, I haven't seen my son or grandchildren for over twenty years. I probably have great grandchildren I've never seen."

"But everyone here thinks of you as their grandmother. So you have lots of grandchildren you see all of the time," Rachel argued.

"True. But they aren't my own flesh and blood. Don't think I'm not grateful or that I'd change one minute of it. But it's only fair to warn you."

"Where would Juner be without you? Or half the valley, if you'd gone to Texas? I think Billy Bob was being selfish!"

"Not really. He had his life to live and his family to

90

think of. I just want you to know that doctorin' limits your choices."

"I don't care! I like what I'm doing. It feels right. Maybe I won't get married. Won't be anybody left to marry anyway, if this war keeps on. Maybe I'll just have the whole valley for a family like you do."

Granny Sharp smiled and shook her head at Rachel's youthful innocence. "I guess I hoped you wouldn't listen. Still yet, you shouldn't think everyone counts me as family."

"What do you mean? Everyone comes to you for help. I've never heard anyone say a bad word about you."

"Folks don't speak of the devil for fear he'll hear and harm them. There are folks hereabout who believe I get my power of healin' from the devil."

Rachel sat in shocked, unbelieving silence.

"Why?" she finally croaked.

"Superstition. Ignorance. Fear. For whatever reason, some folks believe me to be a witch. But they come to get healed anyway when they hurt bad enough. They'll say the same of you."

"That's stupid and silly! I'll make anybody who says you're a witch eat their dirty lies! I-I-I'll—" Rachel was beating her clenched fists on her knees. She was so mad she wanted to punch someone. How dare anyone say such horrible things about Granny Sharp! How could anyone be so stupid?

"Calm down, Rachel." Granny Sharp's voice cut through her anger. "Years ago it used to hurt me, but it doesn't anymore. Right now, you look like a witch who might fly off even without your broomstick."

"I'm sorry," Rachel said, shamefaced. "I'm trying to learn to control this temper. It doesn't always work."

91

"Keep tryin'," Granny Sharp advised with a twinkle in her eyes. "Just don't keep any black cats or make any hex signs or you'll make these folks certain-sure you're the devil's apprentice."

"I don't know any hex signs and my cats are yellow-striped," Rachel assured her.

"Good. I'll show you the hex sign so you'll know not to do it by mistake ever. That is, if you're sure you want to go on workin' with me?"

"I'm sure," Rachel answered firmly.

That had been a whole year ago. Since then Rachel had become a familiar figure, thundering up and down the hollows and hills astride Bright Star as, more and more, Granny Sharp depended on her to serve the scattered mountain people.

Rachel had never regretted her decision. Yet, for some reason she could not put her finger on, this second spring she had felt unsettled and restless.

Now that the late spring had finally decided to stay, Rachel and Juner were starting out to replenish Granny Sharp's herb supply.

"Hurry on, Miss Rachel," Juner urged from the back of his mule. "You be wool gatherin' agin."

Rachel came to with a start. "Come on, Star." She gave Star a nudge and flew past the startled Juner, calling over her shoulder, "Race you to the cherry trees!"

Juner's mule was no match for the fleet Star. By the time Juner arrived at the cherry trees Rachel had collected the required bark and was ready to go.

Jason was waiting for Rachel on Granny Sharp's front porch.

Looking at Jason's solemn face, Rachel feared the worst. "What's wrong? Is it Grandy? Manda?"

"No. They're fine. It's Matt and Pa. Pa brought Matt home. He's dead, Rachel. Pa's more'n half dead hisself. He's all shot up—an-an. . . ." Jason couldn't go on, his tears choked him.

"Oh, Jason. I'm so sorry. What can I do to help?"

"G-Granny Sharp's already gone over. I stayed to bring you and Juner." Jason wiped his eyes and started for his horse.

Juner laid a big hand on Jason's shoulder. "Juner's sorry, Jason. Juner liked Matt. He was nice. Juner's sorry."

"Thank you kindly, Juner."

All three mounted and rode off into the early spring darkness to bury the first Carder casualty of the war.

Two weeks later Jason rode over to say good-bye.

"Pa's mendin' now. I'm gonna go find Andrew. Me and him are gonna fight together till this war's over." Jason's mouth was set in a grim line.

"You know where to look for Andrew, Jason?" asked Manda.

"Last Pa heard he was up in Maryland with the Ninth Cavalry."

"Maryland's a far piece. Ride wary, Jason!" Grandy said. "Come back to us, boy."

Jason's grin broke through. "Oh, I aim to, Grandy. Got to have me some more of Manda's blackberry pies 'for I die."

Rachel flung her arms around a startled Jason and kissed him.

"I'll miss you so much, Jason. Do you have to go?"

Jason gave her a quick hug and vaulted into Cherokee's saddle before anyone could see his tears.

"Aye, Rachel, I must go find Andrew. And I-I want to fight for the Union. Mr. Lincoln is right. We are One!"

"Aye, Jason. That we are!" Grandy said softly.

Rachel and Jason exchanged looks. Now they were sure which side Grandy favored. It was a strange position, being in a southern state and holding to the Union, yet the majority of mountain men were of this opinion.

Bolstered by Grandy's approval, Jason squared his shoulders and rode off across Little Stoney. Rachel, Manda, and Grandy watched him until he was out of sight.

As the summer wore on, Rachel missed Jason even more than she had thought possible. There were no other young people close by to even talk to, much less to ride with or laugh at. Jason had left a big hole in her life. Rachel became in turn snappish, absent-minded, nervous, or dreamy.

"What in thunder ails Rachel? I've told her a hundred times to close that corral gate! She either smiles at me and says 'Yes, sir', or snaps 'Did!' Gate still stays open—either way!" Grandy demanded.

"She's restless as a willow in a windstorm. That's for sure," Manda replied knowingly.

"She sick or somethin'?" Grandy was still puzzled.

"Not exactly, Jonathan; she's seventeen."

"Seventeen! What's her age got to do with it all?"

"Ah, old man! Have you forgotten what it's like to be seventeen? It's a misery!"

Jonathan looked at Manda as if she were daft. Seeing she was serious, he tried to get more information.

"She's not sick then?"

"No. Nothing that won't pass with time. Just bear with her a mite," Manda advised.

"Good! I was worried about the child." Jonathan decided to act as if he understood what Manda had said.

"Child?" Manda was amused. "Have you looked at Rachel lately? Really looked, Jonathan?"

"Are ye daft, woman? Of course, I've looked. I see her every day—same as you!"

"Come here, Jonathan. Here comes Rachel from the springhouse. Tell me, what do you see?"

Jonathan looked out the window as Rachel came from the springhouse with the butter and milk for their supper.

A light breeze blew Rachel's long sable brown hair back from her face and molded the gingham dress to her trim figure. Tabby and Smokey, the house cats, came racing toward her, hoping for a taste of milk. Rachel laughed at their silly antics and shooed them away with, "After our supper, you greedy girls!" Then Rachel came on toward the house humming to herself.

Jonathan turned away from the window. "Aye, Manda. Now I see. Why, she's a full-grown woman!" He shook his head. "When did it happen?"

Manda laughed. "Right under our noses, I reckon."

Rachel didn't understand her own self. She only knew that one minute she was happy, the next sad. Or, she was all full of energy and enthusiasm about some task—only to find herself lost in a daydream right in the middle of it. She wanted something, but didn't know what it was.

I must be going daft. It's a wonder Granny Sharp or anyone else puts up with me, Rachel mused, as she rode home in the late summer twilight. Today, I spilled the water. Handed Granny Sharp cherry leaves when she wanted sassafras. Burned my finger and cried like a baby! Nothing has gone right this livelong day. It must be this stupid war.

11

Death had never been a stranger to the mountain valley. But in the harsh winter months of 1864, death was a constant companion.

Deep snows and weeks of below freezing temperatures came in November isolating people in their cabins. Virtually nothing moved in the frozen white wilderness. Food and firewood ran out for some families whose men were away fighting. Those families froze or starved to death. Colds, flu, and lung fever ran rampant through the crowded cabins. The strong survived. The weak died and were placed outdoors wrapped in blankets, awaiting a thaw so they could be decently buried. The number of blanket wrapped mounds grew larger and larger.

Rachel, who usually was thankful for the protection and isolation of the mountains, now found herself hating them.

"If we had decent roads and weren't so scattered about, I could get out and help," she fumed for the hundredth time. "These mountains are like a cup. Snow just fills up the cup and never thaws or melts!"

"It'll melt in God's own time," Grandy assured her.

"Humph!" was Rachel's only reply.

When a dim, watery sun finally broke through the clouds and the temperature rose above freezing, Rachel's gloom began to fade. All day long she went from window to window watching the slowly melting snow drip from the roof. Even Manda's cautioning couldn't dampen her rising spirits.

Before breakfast the next morning, a snow-covered, blue-faced, panicky Juner burst into the cabin.

"You got to come quick, Miss Rachel! Granny Sharp's awful sick. She's talkin' outta her head. Wants us to go campin' in a tent! Juner don't know what to do."

Rachel didn't waste time asking questions. She threw on every piece of warm clothing she possessed and followed Juner.

Juner bulled his way through the snowdrifts. When they were too deep for Rachel and she floundered, Juner hoisted her to his shoulders and carried her as he had done years ago.

Spurred by Juner's urgency and her own fear, Rachel hardly noticed the biting, numbing cold. All that mattered was getting to Granny Sharp.

When they reached the cabin, Juner deposited her gently and collapsed in a heap by the banked fire.

The sound of Granny Sharp's labored breathing filled the cabin.

For a moment Rachel was paralyzed with cold and fear. She stood as if rooted to the floor, feeling helpless and inadequate.

A low moan from Granny's sleeping quarters spurred her into action.

She knew she couldn't move Juner so she did the next best thing. She tugged off his wet coat and boots, covered him with a few blankets and built up the fire.

Satisfied she had done her best for Juner, she turned her attention to Granny Sharp.

Granny's frail body was burning with fever. Each breath rattled painfully through her congested lungs. She didn't respond to Rachel's voice, but her feisty spirit fought bravely on.

For a moment Rachel couldn't think what to do. Then Juner's words came back to her . . . "Granny's outta her head. Wants to go campin' in a tent!"

Laughing with relief, Rachel set to work.

"Granny's crazy like a fox, Juner," she said to his sleeping figure. "She wasn't too sick to tell us what to do. You just didn't understand."

Rachel made a tent over Granny's bed with a rope and a blanket. While the warming stones were heating in the fire, Rachel crushed camphor and ditty leaves in a big wash basin. When the stones were hot she lifted them into the basin with the coal shuttle and lugged the basin over to the tent. Once inside, Rachel poured cold water over the hot stones. The result was an aromatic steam that filled the tent. Several hours later, Granny's breathing began to ease a bit.

For twenty-six hours Rachel and Juner worked to bring down Granny's fever. At last Granny fell into a light but easy-breathing sleep.

"I'm so tired, Juner, even my hair aches," Rachel sighed as she put her head down on the puncheon table.

"You sleep a while, Miss Rachel. Juner'll watch out for Granny."

The rest period didn't last long. Thirty minutes later Rachel awoke at the sound of heavy boots stamping on the front porch.

Rachel's heart leapt in fear. Every time someone came from "outside," Rachel feared they would bring news of Jason's death. She struggled to conquer her fear and sleepiness and went to unlatch the door.

Grandy stepped in bringing a swirl of snow and ice with him.

"Bless be, if it's not snowing agin'," he said, stripping off layers of clothes. "How's Granny Sharp?"

"She's breathing easier now. Juner's with her. What are you doing out in this weather?" Rachel scolded as she led him toward the kitchen fire.

Grandy chuckled. "You sound just like your grandma, lass. I come down to give you a spell of rest. Looks needed, too. Run along with ye! Me and Juner will manage whilst you sleep."

Rachel didn't need to be told twice. She was asleep before her head hit the pillow.

The next few weeks rushed past. Christmas came and went without much notice. Uncle Roscoe and Aunt Rose came over for Christmas dinner. So did Uncle Lem and Aunt Martha. Talk was strained. It was hard to be jolly under the threat of the seemingly never-ending war. Everyone left as soon as possible after dinner.

The January thaw, which usually came in the first weeks of the new year, didn't come until the last week of January. Nevertheless, the sun and warm wind melting the winter's snow were a welcome sight. Even the sea of brown mud caused by the melting snow was a welcome change from the eternal blanket of white.

Rachel was spending a rare day at home with Manda.

Even though Granny Sharp had recovered from her bout with "lung fever," she was unable to go out on sick calls. Rachel and Juner had been kept busy every day riding all over the valley delivering medicine and comfort.

Sitting in the sunny kitchen sipping hot sassafras tea, Rachel sighed in pure content. "I reckon everyone decided to take a day off from being sick to enjoy this sunshine. I sure am glad. I've been on Star's back so much lately I was afraid I might be growing onto the saddle!"

"You and Star both have earned a restin' spell," Manda allowed. "Don't count on it being a long rest. Old Man Winter isn't near gone yet. This thaw is only a teaser."

As if to make her warning come true, a knock sounded at the front door.

"Oh, Lordy! Should have kept my thoughts inside, I reckon. You just sit. I'll get it," Manda said, heading for the front door. Manda opened the door.

A tattered, mud-spattered man leaned against the door frame.

"Mornin', Miz Carder," the muddy scarecrow said.

"Mornin'," Manda said, peering at the man more closely. "Lonnie? Lonnie Campbell?"

"Yes, ma'am. What's left of me under the mud." He sagged more against the door frame but managed a weak grin.

"Well, don't just stand there grinnin' and about to drop in yore tracks. Come on in!" Manda tried to pull Lonnie in the door.

"I'm too muddy to come in that-a-way, Miz Carder," Lonnie protested, holding back. "I'll come around the back. And if you'd give me a pan o' water and soap, I'll wash up and come in."

Manda gave in. "You could use a wash up, that's for

sure, Lonnie. I'll have your water waitin' when you get there."

A somewhat cleaner Lonnie Campbell joined Rachel and Manda in the kitchen a few minutes later.

Rachel had never seen a man so thin. He had so little flesh on his bones that he looked like a walking skeleton. That he was sick and exhausted was obvious. He was also starving. He wolfed down the eggs, ham, biscuits, and gravy that Manda had fixed for him.

"I ain't laid my eyes on sich as this since I left home! Lordy, Miz Carder, I eat anymore I'm apt to bust," Lonnie said, declining a second helping of eggs.

"You could use some meat on those bones, Lonnie. You're skinny as a rail. But I 'spect you need a good night's sleep even more. You finish your milk, and Rachel will have a bed all ready for you," Manda said firmly.

Lonnie pushed back from the table with an effort. "Nothin' I'd like better, Miz Carder. 'Ceptin' to get on home. I'm goin' on up to Piney Ridge as fast as I kin make it. It's been more'n two years since I seen Betsy or the young'uns. I *got* to git home!" A note of desperation crept into Lonnie's voice. He stood up preparing to go. "Onliest reason I stopped by was to git word to Roscoe that I seen his boys, Jason and Andrew, at the Battle of Nashville. They's both well and doin' good then."

"Jason? You saw Jason? When?" Rachel was so happy she forgot all about how weak Lonnie Campbell was and gave him a hug that nearly toppled him to the floor.

"Whoa, now, Miss Rachel." Lonnie laughed and regained his balance. "Y'all hadn't heard about the Battle of Nashville?"

Manda and Rachel shook their heads impatiently.

"There was some fearsome fightin' goin' on. 'Bout

December fifteenth or sixteenth, I reckon. I was paroled out. On my way out of Nashville, who do I see walkin' sentry duty but young Jason! He knowed I was comin' home and he sent word to say him and Andy was fine. Gonna be stationed in Nashville for a while."

Rachel burst into tears and fled to her room.

Manda got Lonnie on his way with the loan of a horse and a sack of "goodies" for his family. Then she went upstairs to see about Rachel.

"Rachel, honey, you all right?"

Rachel sat up on her bed, drying her eyes. "I'm fine, Manda."

"I'm right sorry about all that fightin' in Nashville, honey. I know how I'd feel if the place I'd lived in most of my life was all torn up by a war," Manda said as she smoothed Rachel's rumpled hair.

"Oh, Manda, I wasn't cryin' over Nashville! I was just happy to hear Jason was alive. I've been so afraid every messenger would bring word of his death."

"I know, I know, honey," Manda soothed.

"No, you don't!" Rachel sobbed. "Jason's been my only true friend up here and he left me. I—I've missed him so!"

"Friends are worth your tears, Rachel," Manda said gently. "I 'spect we've all missed Jason more than we admit. He's special. He could always make folks laugh—at him or with him."

"Yes," gulped Rachel, drying her eyes. "Jason always sees the funny side of everything. It's hard to picture him mad enough to fight anyone. I've tried, but I can't. That's what makes it so hard."

"Oh, Jason can be tough when he thinks it's necessary. Once, when he was about five, his favorite pup took sick.

Bad sick. Roscoe was going to put him out of his misery, but Jason said no. He grabbed his pa's gun and stood guard over that dog all day. That night he snuck off and carried that pup all the way down to Granny Sharp's. 'Bout five miles in the dark and that dog weighed as much as Jason did. Lordy, was Granny surprised at what come to her door! She tended that dog for two days and it got better, too. Best herd dog they ever had."

By this time, Rachel was smiling. She could picture the miniature Jason holding off his whole family while he tended his dog.

"That must have been Nipper. Jason used to talk about him all the time."

"That's the one." Manda laughed. "Jason and Nipper could get into and out of a peck of trouble. Dog's long gone but I reckon Jason can still take care o' hisself. Leastwise, he's alive and well."

"Thank the Lord!"

"Amen. Now, don't you think you ought to ride over and tell Roscoe and Rose?"

"Oh, my goodness! I forgot about Uncle Roscoe and Aunt Rose! They'll be so happy!"

Rachel threw on her riding clothes, saddled Star, and was off in less than ten minutes, bearing the good news.

12

Manda was right. Old Man Winter wasn't nearly through. February brought two snow and ice storms sealing the valley in again. Blustery high winds were piling up snowdrifts six feet high in some places.

"I'm glad you got that safety line up to the barn 'fore it started driftin'," Manda said, as she helped Grandy off with his boots.

"It keeps up this blowin' we'll have to dig our way out, come mornin'." Grandy took a welcome cup of hot tea from Rachel.

"The horses all right?" Rachel asked.

"A mite skittish at being cooped up so long. But glad enough to be out o' the storm, I expect. It's not a fit night for man nor beast."

They had just finished supper. Grandy cocked his head to one side listening. "Did you hear aught?" he asked Rachel and Manda.

"Nothing but the wind—" Rachel answered.

"Hush, now! There it is again," Grandy said.

Everyone strained to hear any sound besides the wind.

"What did it sound like, Grandy?"

"A horse! Hush, now. . . ."

Faintly, very faintly the whinnying of a horse was heard.

"It's comin' from the front," Manda said.

"Could one of our horses have gotten out?" Rachel asked, as all three of them headed for the front door.

"Not likely. Could be the wind is carryin' the sound round about," Grandy answered, peering through the frosty snow-covered windows. "Can't see a blessed thing!" he growled. "Fetch a lantern and my coat, Rachel. I'll go have a look."

"Best be cautious, Jonathan. Two feet away from the house you could get lost," Manda said as she helped him on with his coat.

"Aye. I'll go easy. But no horse should be out in a' that."

Taking the shielded lantern, Grandy pushed his way out the door.

Manda and Rachel hovered anxiously inside. They could hear nothing but the sound of the howling wind.

In a few minutes, which seemed like an eternity, they heard Grandy's shout for help.

Manda flung open the door and fought her way out to help Grandy with the large white burden he was trying to get to the house. Rachel was right behind her.

The three of them struggled and tugged the frozen lump inside.

"Oh, Lord help us! It's a man!"

"Get him to the kitchen. To the fire!" Grandy ordered.

They half-carried, half-dragged the snow-covered man to the kitchen.

"You see to him, Manda. I'll try to get his horse to the

barn." Grandy pulled on his boots and left Manda and Rachel with the inert body in front of the fire.

"Is he dead?" asked Rachel.

" 'Purty near, I'd say. Heat up some water, Rachel. I'll try to get off his clothes."

The two of them worked swiftly and silently over the still form.

"He's a soldier! A Yankee," Rachel said as they stripped off the sodden blue uniform.

"He's bad wounded, too," Manda observed, peeling off the blood encrusted shirt.

A half hour later they had just finished doing what they could for the unconscious man when Grandy stumbled in the back door exhausted.

Manda thrust a cup of hot tea in his hands and started taking off his coat and boots.

"Did you get his horse to the barn, Grandy?" Rachel asked when she thought Grandy had warmed enough to talk.

"You'll not be believing this—but that horse knew the way better than me! She more or less dragged me up there. Got her inside and rubbed her down good and fed her. Then I took another good look at her. You know what?" Grandy asked with wonder. "That poor, frozen bag o' bones out there—that's Gypsy!"

"Gypsy? Wasn't she part of the herd Uncle Lem sold to the Confederate Army?" Rachel asked, unbelieving.

"Jonathan, are you sure?"

"Aye! I'm sure."

"How do you reckon a Yankee came to be riding a Rebel horse?" mused Manda.

"How did they get here? Why?" Rachel wanted to know.

"Strange things happen in a war," Grandy said. "How bad's the lad hurt? There was blood all over the saddle."

"He's got a side wound and he's lost a lot of blood. He's half-frozen and half-starved. But his pulse is slow and steady and he doesn't have a fever. We'll know more about his chances by morning," Rachel answered.

"Looks like your trainin' with Granny Sharp is goin' to come in right handy," observed Grandy.

"You two go on to bed. I'll stay down here and keep the fire going," Rachel said.

"I'll be down later and take a turn with him," Manda said.

"We'll *all* take turns. You first, Rachel. Manda or me will relieve you in three hours," ordered Grandy.

"That's best, I reckon. Good night, Manda—Grandy." Rachel sat down by the pallet on the floor to keep watch over the wounded soldier.

"His name's Benjamin Allen. He's a captain from the Third Pennsylvania Cavalry," Grandy said at breakfast. "Found his papers in his coat last night."

Manda snorted, "Yon lad hardly looks old enough to be let out alone, much less a captain in the Union Army!"

Rachel got up and peeked at the still form on the pallet. Despite the ragged growth of blond beard the man did look incredibly young.

"Did he ever come to?" Rachel asked.

Manda and Grandy shook their heads.

"Never said a word all night. He groaned some. Never was out of his head though," Manda said.

"Do you think we could get out and get Granny Sharp?" Rachel asked.

"Not a chance. Snow's stopped, but it's drifted up

107

pretty bad. 'Sides, Rachel, you can do as much for him as Granny Sharp could," Grandy said.

Rachel shook her head at Grandy's confidence. "I'm not sure about that, Grandy. I'd like to look at that wound again. It may need some stitches. I'll feel better when Granny Sharp can look at him."

"I think we'd best move him to the sickroom. He can't stay here in the middle of my kitchen," Manda said. "Jonathan, you take his shoulders and Rachel and I will take his feet. The bed's all ready."

With only a little struggling, the three of them managed to get the unconscious Captain Allen into bed in the small room off the kitchen.

"Been a while since we used this room. Used to have one or the other young'un in it most all winter, seemed like. Measles, mumps, croup, colds, one thing or another when they were little," Manda said as she helped Rachel unwind the dressing on the wound. "Kept them here nearby where I was. Room's good and warm from the kitchen, too."

Rachel finished taking off the bandage. "Moving him started the bleeding again." She held the old bandage to her nose and sniffed. "The wound smells clean. No poison's set in. Still, he can't afford to lose more blood. I'd best stitch this up some. Will you help me, Manda?"

"You just tell me what to do, Rachel."

Grandy moved hastily out of the room. "I'd best see to the stock now. You won't be needin' me, will you?"

Rachel looked up. Grandy was a pale shade of green.

"No, thank you, Grandy. You go see about the horses."

After he had gone, Manda chuckled. "Did you ever see the likes o' him? He never has been able to abide seeing someone stitched up. Makes him lightheaded."

"I know just how he feels!" Rachel said grimly. "Still,

it's got to be done. I'll need one of your good needles and some silk thread, Manda."

Captain Allen regained consciousness just before suppertime. His eyes flew open and he looked around slowly. Spotting Grandy, he said, "Where am I?" His voice was so deep and mellow that it would have drawn notice even without the clipped Yankee accent.

"Carder's Cove."

"Um-m . . . smells good." Captain Allen seemed reassured and promptly fell asleep again.

Rachel roused him later to take a few spoonfuls of broth but he seemed to prefer sleep to food.

"Granny Sharp says sleep is nature's best medicine. Captain Allen must believe that, too," Rachel said as she came back to join Manda and Grandy in the kitchen.

Rachel took the last watch that night.

Morning came and found Rachel dozing in the chair beside the sickbed.

She awoke suddenly, feeling as if someone were watching her.

"You look very pretty sleeping there."

"Captain Allen?" Rachel sat up and tried to see through the dim light with her sleep-filled eyes. "Are you awake, then?"

"I think so— else you are a dream—which might well be," he said. "But I hope not."

"How do you feel?"

"Weak and a trifle sore. Definitely not fit to ride out of here." He tried to rise, but fell back with a groan.

Rachel was beside him in a flash. "Don't try to sit up, Captain Allen. You have a bad wound in your side and you've lost a lot of blood. Do you hurt anywhere else in particular?"

109

"My right leg's hurt, I believe. My horse fell on me. I do remember that."

Rachel pulled down the covers and examined the leg carefully. It did seem swollen at the calf.

"You've either a bad bruise or a greenstick fracture. Probably be a good idea to splint it."

"Are you a doctor, Miss?"

"Not exactly, Captain Allen. I do help out where I can. We don't have a doctor hereabouts."

"Could you call me Ben? Captain Allen is so-uh—formal."

"I suppose so." Rachel laughed.

"What may I call you?"

"Rachel. I'm Rachel Car—Sutton." Rachel gave a small laugh at her almost mistake. "I almost said Rachel Carder because I live here with my grandfather and grandmother Carder."

Ben frowned trying to recall something. Then he said with a grin, "Carder's Cove? Is that where we are?"

"That's right."

"I thought I'd dreamed it . . . a tall old man and the smell of ham cooking."

"No, that was Grandy. Do you think you could eat a little? Maybe not ham yet. . . ."

"I do believe I could manage to eat a whole hog if I could stay awake. I'm so sleepy," Ben complained.

"You rest, Ben. I'll wake you when breakfast is ready."

Ben was asleep before she finished speaking.

The next few days brought a great change in both the weather and Ben. The sun came out of hiding and melted even the deepest drifts of snow, exposing tiny green plants all ready for spring. Each day the warm wind and sun coaxed the shoots a little higher. Winter's drab grays and whites were quickly giving way to spring's browns, greens, and yellows. Color had returned to Ben's face, too. His naturally fair complexion had been chalk white from illness and fatigue. Now his freshly shaven cheeks had a rosy tint and his dark brown eyes followed Rachel with lively interest.

"Rachel, do you think I could get up out of this bed today?"

"You know very well what Granny Sharp said yesterday, Ben. Two more days, at least, in bed. Then you can sit up for an hour or so. You don't want to tear loose my beautiful stitches, do you?"

"No, ma'am." Ben sank back resignedly on his pillow. "I hate to be so much trouble."

"You'll be up and around in no time, Ben, if you put your mind to gettin' well and stop frettin'," Rachel scolded.

"Yes, Doctor," Ben said with a false meekness and a sheepish look on his face.

Rachel couldn't help laughing at him. "I'll bring my sewing in here and sit and keep you company. Maybe that will keep your mind off gettin' out of bed."

"I *knew* you were a doctor!" Ben said triumphantly. "That's a perfect prescription for what ails me!"

"Humph! I never heard of company curing a side wound or a broken leg," Manda said from the doorway. "Maybe you've found a new cure, Rachel," she teased.

"Lordy, I'd best get over to Miz Hyder's and see if I can cure her broken hip. Or down to the Smith's and see if Jake's finger will mend. Can't waste this cure on just one sick person, can I?" Rachel jumped up and started from the room.

"You come back here, Rachel!" Ben yelled. "You and Miz Manda are just plain cruel to tease such a sick man."

111

Rachel came back, carrying her sewing. "I'll only stay if you tell us how you came to find us in that storm and all."

"I'll try. I'm not too sure about the last day or so myself," Ben said. "The last part of February, the eighteenth, I think, I was given a squad of new recruits and assigned escort duty to a supply train. This was over in Virginia, near Saltville. On the second day out we got hit by the Rebs. They're fighting with their backs to the wall, you know . . . no food, guns, clothes, or ammunition. But, man, can they fight! Anyway, we chased some stragglers back into the mountains. Got separated from the supply train. Then came the first snow and ice storm. My men and I were lost out there in those mountains with only two days' food for ourselves . . . none for our mounts. The Rebs were sniping at us all the time. They chased us in circles. Wouldn't let us make camp. Picked off my men one by one—took our horses and ammunition whenever they could." Ben's eyes glazed over with the pain of remembering.

"Ben, it's all over now. Don't tell us anymore. Just forget it. You're safe now," Rachel soothed.

Ben managed a hint of a smile. "It's better for me to talk about it, Rachel. I need to remember. It's just—well—some of those soldiers were so young! So green! They'd never been under fire before. Now, I don't even know if any of them ever made it back!"

"How did you get over to Tennessee? We're quite a piece from Saltville," Manda asked.

"Like I said, we were lost, riding in circles. I didn't have any idea where we were. The storm let up some, and so did the Rebs. I had eight men left, counting myself. We'd come to a good-size river and decided to follow it a ways. One of the men said he thought it was the Holston River."

Manda nodded her head. "Probably was."

Ben continued in his low, melodic voice. "We were riding along the river's bank—came to a bend in the river and like a fool I didn't send a scout ahead. We ran right into a group of Reb cavalry camped there. We fought. My horse was shot out from under me. In fact, he fell on me. I jumped up and grabbed a Reb horse as it raced by without a rider. I'd lost my gun. I had no choice but to run. Two Rebs took off after me. That's when I took the bullet. I crossed the river somewhere. Those two just kept after me. I kept going up one mountain—down another. Don't know how that horse kept going. She was a bag of bones to start with. Then came the blizzard. I couldn't find shelter. It was all I could do to stay in the saddle. I gave that horse her head—I don't remember anything after that." Ben sank back on his pillow, exhausted.

"Lucky for you that Gypsy remembered her way home," Rachel said.

"She's your horse?" Ben said in astonishment. "How did she get the name Gypsy?"

Rachel laughed. "Grandy said when she was just a filly she kept running off. Jumped every fence he ever put up."

"I'm sure glad she remembered how to get home."

"Me, too," Rachel said.

"Now it's your turn," Ben said. "Tell me about Carder's Cove."

"What do you want to know?" Rachel asked, puzzled.

Ben looked at her unbelievingly. "For starters—*where* is Carder's Cove? Are you Yankees or Rebels? How do you manage to eat so well? The rest of the South is starving."

"We're in the upper east mountains of Tennessee. We are neutral—neither North nor South. We grow or raise our own food and make do without the rest," Rachel replied.

113

"Neutral? I don't see how—?" Ben said.

Rachel explained to Ben about Jonathan Carder and his sons . . . about the division of the family and how Manda and Grandy had solved the problem as best they could.

Ben shook his head. "I can't believe it! It would never work anywhere else."

"It works here," Rachel said tartly. "Everyone knows Grandy. They know he's as good as his word. Anyone who asks for help here gets it—North or South. We're tucked away in these mountains far from anything either side needs. So no one comes through here fighting. I suspect not too many people—North or South—even know we're here."

"You're lucky," Ben said.

"Yes, we are. But just because we haven't been a battle-ground doesn't mean we haven't had our sufferin', too. We've lost men on both sides in the fighting. We've lost some families, as well. They couldn't make it while their men were gone, even with what help neighbors could give." Rachel's eyes filled with tears, remembering the frozen remains of the Evans family she and Juner had found in the backwoods last winter.

"Don't cry, Rachel. Please don't cry," Ben begged. "The war will be over soon. The South can't hold out much longer. She's whipped, and she knows it. She just won't quit."

Manda had come into the room at the sound of the upraised voices.

"Humph! The fightin' may be about over but I'm a'feared the war will go on for years. Southerners got long memories. Mountain folks, especially," Manda said. "It'll be a long while a'fore this wound heals."

"I hope you are wrong," Ben said. "But I fear you are right. You haven't seen the destruction that's gone on outside these mountains. I heard that General Sherman had burned half the state of Georgia."

"Why?" Rachel demanded.

"To end the war more quickly, he said," Ben answered. "Who knows what generals think?"

"I know what I think," Manda said, looking at Ben's strained face. "I think you need to rest some, Ben. And I need you in the kitchen, Rachel. Jonathan will be hungry as a bear when he comes in. We'd best have something on the table 'sides the plates."

"Come talk to me later, Rachel, when you get a chance," Ben said.

"Talking has tired you out, Ben," Rachel replied.

"Then just come sit beside me. I like looking at you."

Rachel blushed and quickly left the room. Manda chuckled and gave Ben a wink as she left.

That evening, before going up to bed, Rachel slipped into Grandy and Manda's room. It was the only room with a mirror in it. Rachel had looked into it maybe a dozen times before. She'd never really felt the need to know how she looked. Suddenly, she wished she had a mirror in her own room.

She held the lantern up close and studied the face she saw reflected in the mirror: long chestnut brown hair, raven eyebrows and lashes, deep blue eyes, a nose—a little long, perhaps—and a wide mouth set in an oval-shaped face. Nothing much different from anybody else. Still, she thought, I've changed considerable since I came here almost four years ago. And I never even noticed. She looked down at the rest of her body not reflected in the small mirror. I've filled out everywhere, it seems like. Wish I had a big mirror to see how I look all over.

Hearing Grandy and Manda coming up to bed, she

hastily slipped out of the room before they could catch her primping and tease her about being vain.

Still, I'm not ugly. Maybe not pretty. But not ugly either, Rachel thought, as she undressed for bed. Suddenly she picked up her discarded dress and looked it over with dissatisfaction. I wish I had a new dress! A blue one to match my eyes. She laughed at herself and thought, I wonder whatever makes me act so flighty all of a sudden? It must be the spring air!

13

Mother Nature seemed to be apologizing for the long, cruel winter. Blustery, unpredictable March became as mild as May with gentle warm breezes, sun-drenched days, and velvet, star-filled nights. It was so unusual it was unsettling.

It wasn't the weather that unsettled Rachel. It was Ben. Every minute spent with him was a joy. Every minute away from him was a misery. For the first time, Rachel resented her long rides to tend the sick. Yet seeing Ben's eyes light up when she returned was almost worth the pain. It made her tingle all over with happiness. There never seemed to be enough hours in the days that passed so swiftly. Ben's wounds were healing rapidly and that pleased her. Yet she knew that his healing meant he would soon be leaving. The mere thought made her stomach churn and her heart squeeze tightly in her chest. She tried not to think about it.

As for Ben, he hobbled about making himself useful wherever he could. He observed, asked questions and made friends with everyone he met. He adored Manda and felt at ease helping her around the house. Yet his eyes always sought out Rachel. Ben watched her with a growing fondness as she moved through the days with quiet grace, bubbling laughter, hard work, and deep caring for her people. She was as changeable and enduring to Ben as the mountains she lived in. And, if she had to ride out to tend someone, he was uneasy until she returned. The thunder of hooves on the river road always brought him to the front of the cabin where he would wait expectantly for his first glimpse of her.

"She rides like no woman I've ever seen!" Ben exclaimed to Manda one day as Rachel rounded the bend with her hair and her horse flying in the wind.

"She had a good teacher," Manda said proudly.

Ben didn't hear her. He was walking quickly toward Rachel.

Rachel became accustomed to his greeting and dreaded the day he wouldn't be there.

Propriety was always observed. Ben never did more than help her dismount or hold her hand if they were walking. They were never totally out of eyesight or earshot of Manda or Jonathan. It was the mountain custom and rigidly observed.

"It's a bewilderment to me what they find to talk about," Jonathan said, as he watched Ben and Rachel chattering away on the porch one morning.

"You must be gettin' old then, Jonathan." Manda laughed at him. "If you—you dinna' remember your courtin' days."

"Courtin'? Who's courtin'?" Jonathan's eyes widened in surprise.

"Blind as well, are ye? Ben and Rachel can hardly stand to be out of each other's sight. Surely, you noticed?" Manda said.

"Aye, I noticed, Manda. I thought they gleamed each other from the start. I've kept my eye on Ben these past few weeks. Rachel could do worse. Aye, much worse."

"You're an old fox, Jonathan Carder. Had me believing you'd not noticed those two. Do you suppose they know it yet?" asked Manda.

Jonathan laughed. "I'd say each of 'em suspicions it . . . in himself . . . but doubts the other one."

Manda nodded. "I reckon so, too. That's what's makin' 'em so fidgety." She sighed. "Suppose he'll take her off to Pennsylvania?"

"Too early to tell. Ben was studying law 'fore becomin' a soldier. He likes farmin' better, though. Right fair judge o' horses. That accounts for the cavalry, too. Said his pa wanted him to go in the Legal Corps but he held out for the cavalry. Got a mind of his own—Ben has."

Manda snorted. "He'll need it with Rachel, I'll wager."

Jonathan's eyes twinkled. "Aye, she takes after the MacDonalds—your side o' the family."

Manda replied indignantly. "I'll thank you not to bad mouth my family, Jonathan Carder! A case of a pot callin' the kettle black, I'd say." Manda turned and marched stiffly into the house.

Jonathan laughed and called after her, "Always did admire a woman with spirit."

"You best get to work, old man!" Manda sang out.

"Had to have the last word, didn't she?" Jonathan said and headed toward the barn.

Manda hummed to herself as she worked around the kitchen. She hadn't really been angry with Jonathan. She was glad Jonathan liked Ben. It would be more than she could bear to have Rachel end up like Sarah! Rachel might go off to Pennsylvania with Ben—Lordy, how she'd hate to see her go—but Rachel wouldn't go away and never write or visit them again. Come to think of it, she might be crossing her bridges before she came to them. This war seemed like it was going on forever. No one could tell what was going to happen from one day to the next in the best of times, but in this topsy-turvy war even to guess was foolish.

Foolish or not, Manda continued to think about the two men who had ventured beyond the misty mountains and affected her life. Both Ben and Rachel's father, Wesley Sutton, were outlanders, just as she had been many years ago. Why did the two men seem so different? To be sure, Ben was a northerner and Wesley a southerner. But that was only a difference of where you happened to be born. In fact, Ben seemed to fit in better with mountain folk than Wesley ever had. That was part of it, she was sure. Wesley always seemed to be laughing at everyone, except Sarah. He'd found their ways countrified and couldn't wait to get back to the city or civilization as he called it. He was a big talker, Wesley was. A smooth one, too. He'd spun dreams as easily as Manda could spin yarn. That was the part that had riled Jonathan. "A dreamer with an itchy foot" is what Jonathan had called Wesley. That hadn't been quite fair. Wesley was a trader. Oh, he didn't have a store, like Hugh Tipton, or a peddler's pack, like Ole Isaac, but he did make his living trading things. He purely hated farming or staying in one place, he'd said. Handsome enough to catch any girl's eye. But Wesley only had eyes for Sarah and she for him. Well, that was over and done with.

What about Ben? He's been here a little over a month . . . part of that time spent helplessly in bed. Ben's handsome enough in his way—nothing remarkable at all about him till you notice his eyes—large, warm, deep brown eyes that look right into yours with an open friendly gaze. Those eyes and a wide, slow grin make Ben worth a second look. And his voice, so deep, mellow, and surprising coming out of such a lanky frame. Once he got some more meat on that frame he'd really turn a few heads—North or South. Ben isn't much of a talker, more of a listener. He talks when he has something to say. Ben likes people, and he's curious. Seems to be interested in everyone and everything. Lordy, the questions he asks! Maybe that comes from being a lawyer fellow. Anyways, he's got a trade even if he does like farming better. Ben's the settling kind. Rachel deserves that after traipsing all over whilst she was young.

Manda went out on the back stoop to throw out her dishwater. She paused to enjoy the warm spring air and drink in the budding beauty of the mountains.

Off in the distance, Jonathan was repairing the split rail fence. He saw Manda and waved.

Manda waved back. She smiled and gave a small sigh of contentment. "When all's said and done, it's been a good life. Eh, Jonathan?" she said aloud.

The next evening at supper Rachel asked Manda if she and Ben could pack a picnic lunch and ride up to High Meadow in the morning.

"I want to show Ben my most favorite place," Rachel said.

To go off alone together was a definite breach of mountain courtship rules. No decent single girl would do it. But Manda didn't blink an eye. "Don't see why not," she replied, "if Ben feels up to it."

"I'm fit as a fiddle, Miz Manda," Ben replied.

Jonathan pushed back from the table and stood up.

"Reckon I'll go to the barn and finish up the chores 'fore dark."

"I'll go with you, Mr. Carder. I'd like to speak with you, if I may," Ben said.

Jonathan shot Ben a quizzical look and said, "Come along, then."

"I'll get our lunch basket ready. Then we can leave at sunup and have all day," Rachel said.

"First we wash up the supper things, young lady," Manda said as she started to clear the table.

Rachel held up the polished pewter pitcher, trying to see her face in it. "Manda, is my nose too long?" she asked.

Startled, Manda turned and stared at Rachel. Then she laughed and said, "Too long for what?"

"Oh, you know what I mean, Manda. Is it too long? Too long to be uh-uh pretty?"

"Well now, I never thought of noses being pretty," Manda said thoughtfully. "But as noses go—yours is in the right place—and it seems to do its job pretty well.

Oh, Manda, you're teasin' me!" Rachel laughed. "I reckon there's not much I can do about it—long or not. I'm stuck with it."

"Just think how funny you'd look without it," Manda said. "Good thing it is stuck."

Ben and Jonathan returned later to find Manda and Rachel drying dishes amid gales of laughter which they tried to explain. But they couldn't stop laughing long enough to make any sense.

"Bit tetched in the head, I allow," Jonathan said.

"Spring fever!" said Ben, joining in the laughter.

After the supper things were put away, Grandy favored them with a few tunes on his fiddle. Ben's baritone, Rachel's alto, and Manda's surprisingly clear soprano made a nice harmony.

"I don't recollect a prettier spring," Manda said when they were all sung out. "Guess we were makin' a joyful noise unto the Lord for it."

For a few moments they sat in companionable silence and watched the moon rise over Cut-off Mountain.

"Time for bed," Grandy announced. "You two best not sit up jawin' all night if you aim to be off early in the morning."

Ben and Rachel reluctantly took the broad hint and went off to their separate rooms.

Rachel felt as if she were floating. Ben must have asked Grandy's permission to propose to her. And she could tell by the happy music that everything was all right. What's more, she knew what her answer would be. Her heart had been full of happiness when she joined Ben in song tonight. It felt so right! She would follow her heart and the mountain way. Wherever Ben went, she would go. His people would be her people and they would live happily ever after —just like the stories.

Rachel pulled her nightgown over her head and pushed away the flicker of regret that threatened to mar her ecstasy.

"Yes," she whispered to herself, "I will miss Grandy and Manda. And my beautiful misty mountains. And my doctoring. But Ben is worth it. Grandy and Manda have each other. Someone will come along to care for my people. I just know they will!"

Holding on firmly to these thoughts, Rachel fell asleep.

The ragged cadence of hoofs pounding awakened her before the shout.

"Ho, Cabin! Miss Rachel!"

Rachel was at her window before the echo died away. "Who's there?"

Alf Taylor's white, terror-stricken face loomed below her in the moonlight. The plow horse he sat astride heaved noisily.

"Alf Taylor, Miss Rachel. It's my Janey. The baby won't come. Janey's been tryin' all day. Ma Trivette says they're both gonna die. Can you come? I don't want Janey to die. The baby neither, can it be helped!" Alf poured forth in a terrified rush.

"Go saddle Bright Star. I'll be right down," Rachel called.

As she changed into her riding clothes, she heard Grandy go out to help Alf.

Alf Taylor was one of the few young men left in the mountains. It was not by choice. Alf had been born with a clubfoot. In spite of his deformity, he was a cheerful, hardworking man. He and Janey Trivette had married last spring. This was their first child.

Rachel ran downstairs. Ben met her at the door with her medicine bag and her shawl. His eyes were shining with a mixture of love and concern. His lips brushed Rachel's cheek as she hurried out.

"Go with God, Rachel," he said softly.

"Thank you, Ben," Rachel replied gratefully, as she felt Ben's love envelop her like a protective shield.

Alf sat impatiently astride Gypsy as Grandy gave Rachel a leg up on Star.

"Thanks for the loan of a horse," Alf was saying. "I'll get her right back."

"No hurry. Your horse is plum tuckered. I'll see to him. You get along, now. Rachel will do what she can. Don't fash yourself!"

The two riders galloped off into the night. The Taylor cabin was in Little Quail Holler about six miles away.

Talking was impossible at their pace.

Rachel's mind was racing ahead. She had never delivered a baby, although Granny Sharp had told her some of the procedures. Most mountain women delivered without anyone's help. Occasionally, there were some problems and help was called for. Rachel thought over everything she knew. She hoped it was enough. Alf and Janey were two of her favorite people.

The Taylor cabin was ablaze with light. Elizabeth Ann, Alf's older sister, met them in the doorway.

"Janey's fadin' fast, Miss Rachel. She's plum wore out," she said, her eyes full of pity and hopelessness.

Rachel pushed past her and followed the loud moans into the bedroom.

The moans came from a large, rawboned woman bent over the bed.

The white-faced, sweating figure in the bed was silent. Janey was too exhausted to cry out in her pain.

Gently, Rachel moved Miz Trivette aside so she could examine Janey.

"She's dyin'! No use goin' after you. I told him so. Alf should'a got a preacher," wailed Miz Trivette.

Rachel ignored her. Calmly and quickly she examined Janey. All the while she spoke softly and reassuringly. "There now, Janey. Just relax a little. Let me have a look-see."

Under her calm ministrations, Janey did relax a little.

"How long have you been in labor, honey?"

"Since about four yesterday. Warn't bad at first. Bad now!" Janey gasped as another contraction swept over her.

"She's dyin'. My baby girl is dyin'. She's payin' for her sin. Oh, Lord. I told her not to marry a man marked by the devil. Yes, I did. Would she listen? Oh, no. Now she's dyin'," Miz Trivette wailed louder in a voice that rose and fell hysterically.

"Alf's not marked, Ma!" Janey found the strength to retort.

"Of course not," Rachel assured Janey. She shot a warning glance at Miz Trivette. "You're having a hard time because the baby's turned wrong."

"It's a sign! God's punishin' you," shrieked Miz Trivette.

"Be quiet, Miz Trivette," Rachel ordered as another contraction tore Janey from her grasp.

"She's dyin'! Oh, Lord, make it quick. Don't let her suffer so."

"Easy now, Janey. I'm going to give you a little something to ease the pain. Don't push anymore. Try to relax. All right?"

Janey nodded. Her tired eyes held a glimmer of hope. "Can you help?"

"I think so. Now drink this and do as I tell you," Rachel said, handing Janey a cup of water laced with a tiny bit of laudanum.

"Only God can help her now. Janey, have you made your peace with God? Have you confessed your sins and asked Him to forgive you? Have you. . . ."

Rachel's temper snapped, as she saw Janey quailing in fear. Eyes blazing, Rachel grabbed the larger woman by the shoulders and shook her.

"I told you to be quiet! You're hurting, not helping. Now, get out—stay out—and shut up!" Rachel ordered as she propelled Miz Trivette through the door.

"Alf, keep this woman out here and keep her quiet, even if you have to gag her. Elizabeth Ann, bring me a pan of hot water, a piece of lye soap, and a dish of lard. Hurry now. We've got a baby to deliver." Not even waiting to see if her orders were carried out, Rachel returned to soothe Janey.

Janey gave her a faint, thank-you smile.

Rachel's blinding fury vanished in an instant. She gave Janey a wink.

Elizabeth Ann silently brought in the things Rachel had asked for.

"Thank you, Elizabeth Ann. You go calm Alf and Miz Trivette down some. Janey and I have some work to do."

Awed, Elizabeth Ann nodded and left. Rachel began scrubbing her hands and arms with hot water and lye soap, all the while talking soothingly to Janey.

"You're a strong, healthy girl, Janey. You just hold on a little longer. I'm going to wash up and grease my hand and I'm going to turn that little Taylor baby around. Then the rest will be up to you. Why, I bet once it's turned, it'll pop out like a grape from its skin. You save up all your strength for that final push. You hear?"

Janey nodded. The laudanum was relaxing her.

"You want a girl or a boy?" Rachel asked. She didn't want Janey too relaxed.

"Don't matter. Long as the baby's healthy."

Asking questions and working between Janey's contractions, Rachel slowly managed to turn the baby's head down in the birth canal. Carefully, Rachel checked to see if the cord was around the baby's neck. If it were, all of her efforts would have been in vain, at least for the baby.

Rachel didn't feel the cord.

"Janey, when the next pain comes, I want you to push as hard as you can," Rachel said, brushing the sweat off her brow with her sleeve.

Silently, Rachel waited and prayed.

The pain came and Janey bore down with all of her remaining strength.

A few minutes later Alf Taylor heard the feeble wail of his first child.

Rachel came to the door, smiling. "If you'll bring me some more water, you can hold your baby girl in a second or two. Mama and baby are both fine."

Elizabeth Ann jumped to get the water.

Miz Trivette simply stared open-mouthed.

Alf blinked unbelievingly for a moment before his face broke into a wide, happy smile. "Janey *and* the baby are all right?"

Rachel nodded and disappeared into the room with the water.

A short time later Rachel brought out a wrinkled, red-faced, crying bundle and placed it in Alf's arms.

"There she is, Alf. She's little and she's perfect! You can go see Janey now, but don't stay long. She's very tired."

Alf handed the baby back to Rachel and limped quickly into the bedroom. Tears streaked down his cheeks unchecked.

Rachel went over and placed the baby in Miz Trivette's arms. "Here's your new granddaughter."

"I-I don't know what come over me," Miz Trivette said, with her face flaming. "I'm powerful sorry."

"I'm the one who should apologize, Miz Trivette," Rachel said hastily. "I lost my temper. As you know, it's a curse all of us Carders have to bear. I hope you'll forgive me."

"No need, Miss Rachel," Miz Trivette said, her hawk-ish face breaking into a smile. "Sometimes a body needs a touch of righteous anger to bring them to their senses."

"Would you like a cup o' coffee?" Elizabeth Ann asked shyly. "We been savin' it to celebrate, Miss Rachel."

"I'd love a cup," Rachel replied. It still embarrassed her when people her own age called her "Miss Rachel." She knew it was a measure of respect but it still made her uncomfortable.

Alf came out and joined the three women. "She's sleepin' now. Fell asleep whilst she was talkin'," he said.

Rachel rose and stifled a yawn. "I'd better be going. Manda will be anxious to hear the news."

"I'll ride over with you and fetch ole Suzy," Alf offered.

"Never mind that. You can bring Gypsy back later today. You need rest as much as Janey does," Rachel said, gathering her things.

Alf walked out with her.

"We're beholden, Miss Rachel. I know they both woulda' died without you. I'm awful glad you came to these mountains. We need you," he said humbly.

"I'm glad I could help, Alf. It pleasured me." Rachel gave the standard mountain answer, but it was heartfelt.

"Janey gave me a message for you," Alf said with a happy grin. "The baby's name is Rachel Elizabeth. The first of many hereabouts, I allow."

"I'm really pleased, Alf, and honored. I'll always remember Rachel Elizabeth because she was the first one," Rachel said. "You come by, if you need me."

"I will."

"You take good care of Janey and little Rachel, you hear?"

"I hear." Alf laughed. "Wouldn't want that Carder temper loose at me."

Rachel shook her head and laughed. "You are so right, Mr. Taylor. See that you remember!"

"I will."

Rachel wheeled Star about and trotted off just as the sun was coming up.

At the crest of Tompert Knob, she halted Star to watch the sun sweep away the shadows and gauzy mist. Dew sparkled like diamonds on the new grass and leaves. Flowers opened and turned toward the sun. The chirp and twitter of birds echoed through the hills. Another day had begun.

A deep feeling of joy and a wave of unutterable sadness swept over her.

How was it possible to feel so happy and so miserable at the same time?

Last night she had gone to sleep happy, with everything settled in her mind. Yet, from the moment she'd seen Janey in pain and known she could help, her plans had been in doubt. Handing Alf his live, perfect baby girl and hearing Alf say: "I'm glad you came. We need you," had sealed her fate. She could not leave, not only for the sake of her people, but for herself.

"Mama and Papa had a dream for me," she told Star. "They wanted a life of leisure and pleasure for me. And I could have that with Ben. I want to marry Ben. I love him so much. But I can't do as a wife should and leave my people when they need me. I don't want to."

Bright Star whinnied in sympathy at the distress in Rachel's voice.

"How do I explain that to Ben? How do I tell him how much I love him and then tell him I can't leave here?"

There was no answer to her question.

Rachel nudged Star into a walk and rode home.

14

"I don't want to go to bed and rest," Rachel said stubbornly. "I want to go on a picnic!"

"You've been up all night," Ben protested.

"I'm not tired. We deserve this one day," Rachel said, her mouth set in a firm line.

"You'd best pay heed when she looks like that," advised Grandy.

"High Meadow is too far to go now," Manda said practically. She knew something was wrong with Rachel and that she needed time alone with Ben to settle the matter. "Why don't you take a picnic down to Three Oaks. That's closer and the trail's clear."

"Aye, that's a good compromise," Grandy replied with a twinkle in his eye that only Manda noted.

"All right. Three Oaks then," Rachel agreed. "I'll go freshen up and pack us a lunch, then we'll be off."

"I don't have a horse," Ben said.

"You can ride Folly," offered Grandy. "She's a mite

high strung so I didn't give her to Alf last night. I figure you can handle her.

"Thanks. It'll be a pleasure to ride another of your horses, Mr. Carder. Most Carder animals do seem high spirited," Ben said with a grin.

Jonathan let out a whoop of laughter. "Aye," he said. "You're right smart for a Yankee."

"I had the good sense to come south, didn't I?" Ben retorted.

"Fate or sense, I'm glad you come," Jonathan said, clamping on his hat. "Have a good time today, you two."

A distressed look flashed across Rachel's face but she answered brightly, "We will, Grandy." And she meant it. The memory of this day would have to last her a long time and she meant to make it a good one.

A split rail fence encircled the meadow at Three Oaks. On the west side the meadow sloped upward to a small hill crowned with three massive oaks and a smattering of dogwood and redbud. Only the chimney stones remained to show that a house had also once crowned the hill. Jonathan Carder had bought the place from the Mullins family when they were burned out and had decided to move west rather than rebuild. Now the land was used only as a pasture for Carder horses.

"Let's picnic on the hill," Rachel said as she jumped down to open the weathered gate logs. "We can let Folly and Star graze down here."

"Suits me," Ben said. "As long as you don't want to race me up the hill. I'm afraid my legs aren't as good as Folly's."

Ben and Rachel had raced the last quarter of a mile and Folly had won by a nose.

132

"With those long legs you'd probably beat me anyway, even if one is hurt." Rachel laughed.

"My legs aren't too long," Ben protested. "Yours are just short."

"I didn't say *too* long, just long."

"I guess I'm sensitive," Ben said. "People have always teased me about my lanky frame."

"I think your frame's just fine," Rachel said as he put his arm across her shoulders. "See, my short legs and your long ones just fit."

"So they do!"

Walking together silently, afraid to break the spell of their first unity, Ben and Rachel climbed the hill.

Reluctantly, Rachel moved out of the shelter of Ben's arm. "I guess we'd better eat. I'll spread the blanket. Is here all right?"

"Fine. I can see why someone built a house up here. The view is wonderful."

Rachel kept up a steady, happy chatter during their lunch.

"I guess we weren't very hungry," Rachel said, surveying the mounds of food that remained untouched on the blanket. "I'll just pack all this away."

Ben watched her with amusement and impatience. "Rachel, will you sit still and listen to me for a minute?"

Rachel dropped the napkin she was folding and sat quietly.

Ben moved over beside her and took her small, tanned hand in his.

Rachel looked at their entwined hands. She could not look into Ben's brown eyes or all would be lost.

"I talked with your grandfather last night. I'm about to leave."

Rachel made a sound of protest.

"You know I must, Rachel. My side is healed and my leg gets stronger every day. I don't want to go. You know that, too. But I must rejoin my unit and get word to my folks that I'm alive."

Rachel made one final effort. "You're still walking with a limp. What if you lose your horse? You'd be on foot. . . ."

Ben put his fingers over Rachel's mouth and tilted her face up toward him. "Hush now. Let me finish."

Rachel nodded, pulling her eyes away from Ben's.

"As I said . . . I spoke to Jonathan last night. I told him I was leaving and asked his permission to speak to you." Ben paused and took a deep breath. "Rachel, I love you. Do you love me?"

Rachel lifted her tear-filled eyes to Ben's. It didn't seem fair to have just found happiness and have it snatched away in the same moment. Yet she had wanted to hear him say he loved her. And she desperately wanted him to know that she loved him.

"Oh, yes, Ben. I love you with all of my heart," she whispered.

"Hoo-ee!" Ben shouted. Then, noticing the tears, he sobered. "Why the tears, Rachel?"

"Because I love you, Ben. But I can't marry you."

"Why not?"

Rachel's words tumbled out in an effort to make Ben understand. "I love you. I do, I do! But I can't leave here. They need me. What if I hadn't been here this morning for little Rachel? I'd love being in Philadelphia with you. I'd love being anywhere with you. But, I can't. . . ."

"Rachel, listen to me!" Ben interrupted firmly. "You

didn't let me finish the speech I rehearsed all night! You don't have to go anywhere. If you will, I want you to wait for me till this war's over. I'll come back, we'll get married and settle down right here in Carder's Cove."

"Here?"

"Right here."

"That's not the way it's done," Rachel protested, refusing to believe this miracle. "The woman follows the man."

"Let's put it this way. If a prospector found a gold mine in the mountains, would he expect the gold mine to follow him or would he come back to it?"

"Oh, he'd come back for the gold," Rachel answered promptly. "But he'd get the gold and leave again. Why should he stay?"

Ben held her small hands tightly in his and tried desperately to make her understand. "Rachel, you're the main reason I want to come back, but not the only reason. I want to come back here to live because of the place and the people. It's very difficult to explain, but I'll try. People are very different outside of these mountains. A man is measured by what he owns, how rich he is. Everyone is clamoring to get richer and more important. That isn't the way here. You measure people by what they are. There isn't any great rush to get rich, have a better house than your neighbor or to wield power. People are important, not riches. Juner is a good example."

"What about Juner?"

"Well, in Philadelphia he'd be hidden away, put in an institution or treated like an idiot child. Of course, it's evident that Juner's not a normal man. But I've never seen or heard anyone treat him badly. Here, he's treated with respect and given a home, food, and work he can handle. In short, he's given dignity."

"That's only as it should be!" Rachel said, angry at the thought of Juner being hidden away.

"Of course it is. People here take time for other people. They take time to go fishing or hunting or just to look at a sunset. Probably none of these mountain people will ever be rich, not by Philadelphia standards anyway. They have their land, their work, their pleasures, and each other and they're happy! I don't want to spend my life scrabbling after wealth, power, and position!"

Rachel thought of her father, always striving to move up in the world to a position of power and wealth. Suddenly, she understood what Ben was trying to say.

"What about your family? Your law practice?" Rachel asked.

"There are lots of lawyers in Philadelphia," Ben said, laughing. "They'll never miss me. I'm not like you. You'd be sorely missed."

"You wouldn't mind me spending time away from home?"

"I'll mind every minute we're apart, but I promise I'll understand, Rachel."

"What about your family?"

"We'll start our own."

Rachel blushed from her neck to the roots of her hair.

Ben laughed and kissed her.

It wasn't at all what Rachel had expected. Ben's lips were very soft as they brushed hers and flitted over her cheeks, landing gently on each eyelid. When at last Ben found her mouth again, she responded with all the love she felt welling up inside her.

After a few of the most delicious minutes of her life, Ben released her.

Breathless, Rachel sat up and brushed back her hair. "D-do you really want to come back here to live, Ben?" At the moment she would have gone with him anywhere.

"Yes, I do. I want to live with you forever." Rachel's passionate response had shaken him.

"Won't you miss the city? All the music and plays and dances you told me about?" Rachel asked, trying to get control of her racing emotions by talking.

"I never did like crowds. I hate dancing and teas and all of that useless chatter. Are you trying to talk me out of this?"

"I just want you to be sure, Ben. Forever is a long, long time."

"I'm certain sure, Rachel. Are you? It might be a long time to wait."

"I'll wait, Ben. No matter how long."

"I'm finding it very hard," Ben said wryly, pulling Rachel to her feet. "Let's walk around the meadow."

Arm in arm they strolled around the meadow, making plans for their future as if there were no such thing as a war.

When Ben could stand it no longer, he took her in his arms and kissed her again. Only his unspoken but understood promise to Jonathan and the possibility that he might not return kept him from making Rachel truly his own.

"This war won't last much longer, will it, Ben?" Rachel asked huskily when Ben released her.

"Don't see how it could last much longer. It'll seem like forever being away from you, though."

"When are you leaving?"

"In the morning."

"Tomorrow?"

"The sooner I leave, the sooner I can return . . . I hope."

Rachel looked at the sky. Thunder clouds were rising over the distant mountains. "We'd best be headin' home soon, Ben."

"Reckon so."

"I hate to leave!"

Ben pulled her close to him. "I wish we could stay here, too. Wish there was no 'war amongst us,' as you call this fighting. But wishing doesn't make it so. Anyway, this place will always be here—just waiting for us."

They stood for a few minutes soaking up the beauty and peacefulness of the mountain meadow.

"Carry it with you, Ben, wherever you go."

"I will."

Rachel whistled for Star and Folly. Reluctantly they packed up and left the meadow.

Manda wasn't too surprised at Rachel's news. One look at Rachel's face had been enough. Besides, Jonathan had already told her of his talk with Ben. Manda was already sure how Rachel felt.

"I thought love was supposed to take away your appetite," Manda said watching Ben and Rachel putting away large helpings of chicken, potatoes, greens, and cornbread. " 'Pears to me, I've been misinformed or you two are foolin' us."

"Now, Miz Manda, I don't know about Rachel, but I do know I'm not likely to come upon such good food for a while. I'm in love, that's for sure, but I haven't lost all my senses."

Grandy snorted, "Who sez?"

Rachel put down her fork and glared at Grandy. "I notice you've been 'without all your senses' for fifty years or so, and you look right pert to me. Got a healthy appetite, too."

"Mm-m—feisty, too. You'll have to watch that trait in her, Ben."

"I will, indeed, I will, sir. What do you do about it, may I ask?"

Manda inquired, sweetly, "Yes, Jonathan, what do you do about it, pray tell?"

Jonathan pushed back his chair and looked at the three of them innocently. "Why, you just watch, Ben. That's all a man can ever do with a feisty woman. Watch and stay out of her reach." Jonathan ducked as Manda flung a dishtowel at him.

The evening flew by too quickly to suit any of them.

There was a warm wind blowing around the April stars as Ben and Rachel sat on the front porch and planned their future home on the land Grandy had just given them. Three Oaks!

Finally, Jonathan called down to them, "Best come on to bed now. We must make an early start, Ben."

Reluctantly, Rachel and Ben came in and went to their beds—if not to sleep, then to rest and gather courage for the times ahead.

Ben and Grandy rode out at sunup on a bright April morning. Rachel watched until they were out of sight. At the edge of the woods, Ben turned, gave a final wave, then was swallowed by the dense trees.

"Come back to me, Benjamin Allen," Rachel said through her tears. "Please, come back."

15

The thunder of hooves through the April mists alerted them before they heard the call. "Hallo-o-o!"

Rachel and Manda were on the porch by the second call.

"Hallo-o-o! Manda! Rachel!"

Grandy, mounted on the jet black Tam, sailed into the yard like a ghost floating in the air.

"It's over! The war's over. Lee surrendered to Grant on the ninth of April."

"Thank the good Lord for that!" Manda said.

"The ninth of April? That's over a week ago. Where's Ben? Does he know?"

"He knows. We found out at Hugh's store. Word just came in. Ben's gone to join up with a Union troop over at Marion. I'll tell you all I know soon as I stable Tam and wash up."

Rachel's heart pounded with joy and the lump of fear that had settled in the middle of her chest when Ben disappeared from view dissolved a little. "War's over! War's over!" kept singing through her mind as she and Manda prepared Grandy a late supper.

Grandy told them all he'd found out at the general store. It was all second and third hand news. Telegraph wires were down all over, but word had come through at Saltville and riders were sent out with the news.

"Means that the fightin' is over almost everywhere by now, I reckon," Grandy said.

"Fightin's over. Healin' the wounds will take a lot more time, I fear," Manda said.

Rachel had hardly been listening. She was so glad that Ben wouldn't be back on a battlefield killing or getting killed.

"How far away is Marion, Grandy?"

"Two days ride at least. Ben rode out with two other Union soldiers headed that way. He said he'd report to the commander at Marion and try to find his old unit . . . if any are left from it. Try to get word to his folks, too. Won't be easy. Everything's a mess up through northern Virginia. Said he'd be back as soon as he can get released, see his folks, and collect his gear."

"How long will that take, do you think?"

"No way to tell, lass. I'd say no less than two months. More apt to be three."

Rachel's face fell. "Three months? I thought with the war over and all, maybe three weeks."

Grandy patted her hand. "Be patient, Rachel. Ben will be back soon as he can. The good Lord willin'. Now, let's be off to bed. You can help me spread the good news tomorrow."

The April weather turned cold and nasty. Rain came down by the bucketfuls, not gentle showers.

"Won't it ever stop?" Rachel muttered as she took off her dripping cloak and muddy boots.

"If it don't stop soon, I may grow webbed feet like a duck," Manda said, trying to talk Rachel into a smile.

"Everybody's sick—colds, flu, chicken pox, croup. Anything you can think of, we've got. A little sunshine would make everyone feel better," Rachel grumbled, refusing to be cheered.

"Sit and eat some of this hot soup I saved for you. You'll feel better then," Manda said as she placed the steaming bowl before Rachel.

Rachel took a few spoonfuls and pushed the bowl away. "I'm too tired to eat, Manda. Thank you, anyway. I'm going up to bed."

The weather continued to be bad. The news was worse. The news of Lincoln's assassination came the last day of April. Grandy was particularly upset by this.

"That's the worst news yet, Manda. Lincoln was the one man to put this country together again. I don't know what to think now. We'll all pay dearly for that wicked deed."

Manda was exasperated, "Ach, now! What I don't need right now is another gloomy Scot! First, Rachel—now you. Gloom and doom, the both of you. You can both glum over each other, then. I'm off to see Granny Sharp for a spell. Even feelin' poorly, she's better company than you two." Manda threw on her cloak and marched out the door.

Rachel and Grandy were stunned into silence. They watched Manda march to the barn—back stiff, head high in the air, looking neither to the right nor the left. Suddenly, her foot hit an unseen root. Manda tripped and fell face first in a mud puddle. Undaunted, she picked herself up, wiped her face as best she could, and marched on to the barn.

By this time Grandy and Rachel were roaring with laughter. They couldn't stop. They laughed until tears ran down their cheeks. They would stop only to look at each other and start again. Rachel got the hiccups. That was even funnier.

Finally, gasping for breath, Grandy said, "What a woman, that Manda! Feisty as a pup and twice as smart."

Rachel, who was still hiccupping, said, "I wouldn't put it past her to have fallen like that on purpose." She giggled again.

Grandy smiled. "She might at that. Manda's right, lass. We've both been a mite gloomy of late."

Rachel didn't answer right away. She was holding her breath to stop the hiccups. Satisfied that she had them stopped, she said, "I know, Grandy. It's just this weather, people sick, hurt, wounded, and—I miss Ben so. I keep worrying about where he is, what he's doing and everything."

"We know, lass. Waitin' is hard, 'specially when you're young. Frettin' over him won't bring him back any quicker than it brought all the other soldiers in this war back to their loved ones. Won't help mend the country either, I reckon. We'd best put on a cheerful face and stumble through as best we can."

"All right, Grandy. I'll try, if you will."

The next few weeks required all of their best efforts. Men began to trickle home from the war. Fewer men came back than had left. And those that returned were not the same. Not all were wounded, minus a leg or an arm, although quite a few were. But all of them, Yanks or Rebs, were changed. They had left as beloved sons or husbands and came back as strangers. It was an unsettled time for everyone.

One bright May morning, Juner came for Rachel and Manda. Granny Sharp had died in her sleep. Manda and Rachel went down and prepared her for burial. Jonathan sent Juner out to tell the sad news.

Two days later, over a hundred mountain people gathered to pay their last respects to their doctor and friend for nearly fifty years. Jonathan preached the sermon and they laid Granny Sharp to rest in a clearing on a hill beside her little house.

Juner went to live with Roscoe and Rose Carder. He would be welcome there. Uncle Roscoe had never fully recovered from his war wounds. Juner would be a big help to them until Andrew and Jason returned.

In her will, Granny left all her medicines and "all her people" to Rachel Sutton, "an apt pupil, with a loving heart and a healing touch." Her house and land were left in trust to Juner, to be used by whoever cared for him.

John Carder, Uncle Lem's oldest boy, came back minus one arm. He left it in Chattanooga, he said. John was a very bitter Rebel. "Lee may have surrendered, I didn't. Fought right on till I lost my arm." John was never going to forgive and forget. He had a stump of a left arm to keep his hate alive.

John and Mark had marched off to war together. But they were soon separated. No one had heard of or seen Mark since the early days of war. Aunt Martha still believed he was alive and would come marching home one fine day. Uncle Lem had almost given up hope.

Rachel was tired. Tired clear down to her bones. Keeping up with the spring chores around the home place was a full-time job. Now, added to that, Rachel had assumed the full title and responsibility of doctor for the valley. This spring there were many calls for her services. Rachel wasn't entirely sure of her craft. She wished she'd had more time with Granny Sharp. She wished she knew more. So many ailments could not be cured . . . just treated and left to nature. Worry over these problems made Rachel even more tired.

"Rachel, you go on up to bed now. I'll clear up these supper things. You look ready to drop in your tracks," Manda said one evening in early June.

Rachel had only picked at her food. She looked up from her plate and gave Manda a smile.

"I'm fine, Manda. A little tired, maybe. I'll help clear and go straight to bed. I promise."

" 'Pears to me you could use some of your own medicine. A spring tonic," Grandy offered.

Rachel looked at these two people so dear to her. Even in the soft lantern light, she could see the lines of age etched in their faces. Why, they're old! When did they get old? she thought. I never even noticed. And they are worried over me!

Smiling, she said, "That stuff tastes awful! Doctors shouldn't have to take their own medicine. That's not fair! But, maybe, you're right. I'll take a big helping of sulphur and molasses before I go to bed. It will either cure or kill me."

"That's a brave lass!" Grandy said, with a twinkle in his eye. "Make you hesitate before you give that slop to someone else."

Whether it was the sulphur and molasses, or the good news that Jason and Andrew had come home, which Uncle Roscoe rode over to tell them, Rachel never knew, but she did feel better the next day.

Uncle Roscoe asked them to supper that night.

"Y'all best come hungry, too. Rose is cookin' enough to feed fifty."

"We'll bring our appetites, never fear," Grandy said.

"Could I bring a little something to help out?" Manda asked.

"Lordy, no! Rose said to tell you to just bring yourselves. Help us celebrate."

The supper was delicious. And there was enough to fill even Juner to the brim.

Rachel ate until she felt like a stuffed turkey. Then she sat back and watched the others. Jason and Andrew looked healthy and well fed. They were full grown men now—both over six feet tall. Both were laughing and happy at the moment, but they had the same withdrawn look in their eyes that she'd noticed in every man who'd come home. She could hardly wait to talk to Jason alone. Aunt Rose and Uncle Roscoe were so happy to have two of their three sons home that it was almost painful to watch them. Manda and Grandy were happy too—with only a touch of sadness that the whole family wasn't present at the celebration. Uncle Roscoe had said hesitantly, "Somehow it wouldn't be fittin' or proper, Pa, to ask Lem and Martha over here when they got Mark still missin', and John bein' so bitter to the Union and all." Grandy had agreed. But you knew it made him sad that the war had split his family apart.

"Penny for your thoughts, Miss Rachel." Jason had slipped up behind her.

"Not worth it, I fear," Rachel answered.

"Good. Don't have a penny, anyway. Come out on the porch and bring me up-to-date on all the goin's on hereabouts."

Rachel and Jason went outside and sat on the front porch. Rachel told Jason about Ben.

Jason gave her a hug. "I'm glad for you, Rachel. You deserve the best. And he'd better be the best or I'll run him right out of here!"

"He is, Jason. I know you'll like him. Now you tell."

Jason's face closed with a snap. "I got nothin' to tell. What I saw I want to fergit. I'll probably spend the rest of my life tryin'!"

Rachel was jolted by the pain and bitterness in his voice. Where was the laughing boy who had left these mountains? Someone had come back calling himself Jason, but it wasn't the same person who'd gone away. Oh, Jason still smiled with his mouth but the laughter never reached his eyes.

"Hey, you two been out there jawin' long enough. Come on back an' be sociable," Andrew said from the doorway.

Obediently, Jason and Rachel went back inside.

Later, on the way home, Rachel sat silent and thoughtful in the back of the buckboard.

She couldn't say she understood the change in Jason because she didn't. Perhaps no one could understand if they hadn't been there. Aunt Rose was so happy because her boys had come home without a scratch. With Jason that was only partly true. Jason had a wound that didn't show . . . unless you'd known him well before. None of her herbs, potions, or salves could cure what ailed him. He was strong. He would recover. But the old Jason was gone forever.

"I'll miss him," she murmured.

147

16

He stood in the doorway, cradling a long rifle loosely in his arms, the ugliest, dirtiest man Rachel had ever seen.

"Howdy, Mister Carder."

They had just finished a quick noon meal before getting back to a late corn planting.

Jonathan went to the open door. "Howdy, Rafe, come on in."

"Hain't time. I cum fer th' yarb woman."

Rachel moved closer to the doorway. The man spoke so strangely, she could make out only a few words.

"Someone up your way need doctorin', then?"

"Yuh, Clem 'n Luke fit. Clem's cut up sum. Maw cain't shet down th' bleeder. Said cum fetch th' yarb wom'n."

Rachel stepped closer despite Manda's restraining hand.

"Where's the cut? How long ago did it happen?"

Squinty blue eyes peered at her out of a grimy, unshaven face. The man looked her up and down slowly before he answered. "Hit's on his rat arm and chest. Happen 'fore sunup. You cum?"

Before Grandy or Manda could say anything, Rachel said, "I'll come. Let me get my things."

Jonathan shook his head, but said, "I'll saddle Star for you."

"I'll help you pack up," Manda said, following Rachel upstairs.

Manda was upset. She told Rachel in no uncertain terms, "You ought not to be goin' up there. They're no-good, no-account white trash!"

"Who are they?"

"The Crows. They live way back in the mountains. There's a whole passel of 'em. All worthless! They keep to themselves . . . not entirely by choice either. They're real mean. Don't allow visitors up on Unaka Ridge. They'll shoot you as easy as saying howdy. Rachel, I don't want you to go up there."

"But, Manda, a man's bleeding to death! I have to go and see if I can help."

"You go up to Crow's Nest and you might never come down again!" Manda retorted. "What if you can't help him? No one can tell what those Crows will do."

Rachel finished packing her satchel and said grimly, "I'll have to chance it, I reckon."

Five minutes later Rachel rode out on Star, following Rafe Crow mounted on a scraggly mountain pony. The pace was a steady and fast one. Rafe rode ahead of her, even though the trail was wide enough for two. He never spoke.

At first, Rachel was on familiar ground. She had traveled most of these hills and valleys with Juner or Granny Sharp in the past few years. But, by late afternoon, she was on totally unfamiliar ground. There wasn't even a trail. Yet, Rafe seemed to be following one mapped in his head. Bushes and trees tore at her clothes and her face. Once or twice, they stopped at a creek to let the horses drink. Rachel had never seen such wild country. One thing for sure, she thought, I'll never get back without a guide.

"Is it much farther, Rafe?" The sound of her voice caused a covey of quail to start out of the brush.

Rafe grinned wickedly at her, showing a mouthful of rotten, stained teeth. "Tard, are ye? Be t'home by sundown." He chuckled. "Clem mought be daid now anyways." Rafe, it seemed, enjoyed other people's misery. They rode on in silence.

Last light was fading in the sky when they came into a small clearing. Their arrival was announced by the baying, yelping, and barking of a host of dogs.

Rafe dismounted, kicked a half dozen dogs away from him, shouting, "Shet yer traps, ye hellers!"

In the dim light, Rachel could make out the outlines of a rude shanty.

A door opened. The doorway was filled by a huge woman, who bellowed, "That you, Rafe? Git that yarb wom'n down hyar. You hear me?"

"Yeah, Maw, I heer ya," Rafe answered meekly.

You'd have to be deaf not to hear her, Rachel thought. She dismounted and moved toward the woman. The woman was huge, weighing two hundred and fifty pounds or more.

"Howdy, Miss Rachel. I be Maw Crow." The mound of flesh rolled aside to let Rachel enter. "Glad you cum. Clem's sinkin' fast. I cain't stanch the flow. This a-way."

As the woman moved away from the door, a terrible odor hit Rachel square in the face. It was like nothing she had ever smelled before—a rotten, pungent odor of un-washed bodies, rotten food, outhouses, dead animals all rolled into one horrible stink. It was all Rachel could make herself do to follow Maw Crow. She felt faint, then realized she'd been holding her breath.

Cautiously, she took a small breath. Though it was still awful, it was the only air she had, so she breathed it.

"Hyar's Clem."

Rachel peered down at the still, pale form on the rude pallet. He looked dead. But Rachel saw a faint pulse at the throat. She bent down and began to pull away the filthy rags covering the wound.

"I need hot water, Miz Crow. Lots of it. And my satchel. And more light." Rachel's voice rang with author-ity. She was no longer a frightened girl, but a healer with a man to save, if possible.

"You heerd her. Move!"

The next few hours whirled by in a flurry of activity. First, Clem had to be stripped of his filthy clothes and the wounds washed so Rachel could see what needed to be done. The chest wound wasn't serious. It only needed clean-ing and stitches. The cut in the upper arm had nicked an artery and sliced through several layers of muscle. Clem was losing a lot of blood from a slowly pumping artery. Rachel considered using a hot iron to sear the wound and seal it off. But, at best, Clem would no longer have use of the arm. At the worst, the wound would putrefy and the arm would have to come off. Rachel could see the nicked artery very well. She had once watched Granny Sharp sew an artery together. She decided to try that method. If it didn't work she could always use the hot iron.

It was a tedious, delicate job. The room was airless and hot. Sweat dripped off Rachel's chin. She kept it out of her eyes by wiping with the back of her arm. She was conscious of other people in the room, but the only sound she could hear was Clem's shallow breathing. At last the job was done. Rachel sat back and looked at her handiwork. Hundreds of tiny stitches inside and out—but no spurting blood. The chest wound only took a few minutes to fix. Already, it seemed that Clem's breathing was easier, although he was still unconscious.

Rachel stood up. Her arms and legs felt like lead. She turned to look at the crowd of people, hovering in the room and doorway.

"That's all I can do tonight. The rest is up to Clem." In spite of herself, Rachel yawned. "What time is it?"

"Past midnight, I reckon," Maw answered. "Shoo! The rest o' you—*shoo*! I'll git you a pallet fixed, Miz Rachel."

Everyone disappeared, as if by magic. Rachel was too tired to inspect the pallet Maw Crow made for her. She flung herself on it and fell fast asleep.

Two things wakened Rachel in the early morning—a growing hunger and a need to use the privy.

Stiffly she got to her feet and went to check her patient. Clem's color seemed some better and he was breathing normally.

Driven by her urgent needs, Rachel tiptoed out of the room and down the dog trot.

A grimy face popped out of a doorway. "Howdy. Whur ya headed?"

Startled, Rachel couldn't understand the words at first.

The rest of the body followed the face. It appeared to be a girl of twelve or so, dressed in a filthy, one-piece sack dress.

"Cat got yer tongue?"

"No. I want to find the outhouse," Rachel replied tartly.

"I'm Zonie. Ain't got one."

Rachel was speechless for a moment. "Well, Zonie where do you go to relieve yourself?"

Zonie giggled and said, "Cum on, I'll show ye. Paw got us'ns a tranch. I'll watch fer ye."

Rachel followed Zonie outdoors and on behind the ramshackle cabin. In the brush, a little way from the cabin, a long, shallow trench had been dug.

"There 'tis. You go. I keep watch." Zonie turned her back on Rachel.

Rachel used the primitive toilet. When she finished, she started back to the cabin.

"Hey! You watch for me now," Zonie said testily.

"Gladly! What do I watch for?" Rachel asked. Zonie giggled again. "Menfolks! They's apt to sneak up on us if we ain't kerful. 'Specially Ephram. He's tetched in the haid anyways."

Rachel could hardly wait to meet this new member of the Crow clan. Everyone she'd met so far was weird; now she learned there was one even more weird. No telling what other surprises were in store for her.

Back at the cabin, Zonie said, "You gwan, I'll brang yer vittles durrickly."

Rachel's stomach hoped that meant food.

Clem was awake and moaning softly when she went back in the room. Rachel checked his wounds again and found the bleeding had stopped. When Zonie brought her food, Rachel sent her for hot water for a poultice and cold water for Clem to drink.

All day Rachel forced sweet sassafras tea down Clem's

throat, whenever he was awake, and even some hot broth at supper. So far, Clem wasn't running any fever and the stitches were holding. Clem had to be kept quiet, so Rachel had slipped a little laudanum into his tea.

A constant stream of people came to peer into the room at Rachel. No one ever spoke. They just stood and stared at her. Rachel soon became accustomed to this attention and ignored them.

Maw Crow brought her supper. "How be Clem?" she asked, bending down to look at Clem's sleeping face.

"He's doing very well. If he will keep that arm still till it heals, he will be all right. If he moves it, he will tear the stitches loose and start it bleeding again. He needs plenty of water, tea, or broth for the next few days. After that he can eat anything he wants."

Maw Crow looked her over carefully. "You done good on Clem. I'm beholden to you. Shuddah ben hyar to holp you today. Had to do some docterin' on Luke, though. Paw whipped him good for cuttin' Clem up that-a-way. Open'd up his back right smart."

Rachel shuddered. She'd never seen a back that had been whipped, but she could imagine what it would look like. "I have some salve here that might help. Would you like some?"

"Naw, thank ye kindly. Luke, he don't need none. He's been whipped s' many times his back's like boot leather." Maw gave a booming laugh at her joke.

Rachel smiled weakly. "I'll leave some herbs for a poultice for Clem and some sassafras for tea. If you keep the bandages clean, he should be fine. I think I could go back tomorrow . . . other folks will be needing me down in the valley."

154

"Rafe'll lead you down cum sunup," Maw said as she rolled her bulk out of the room.

Rachel didn't sleep well that night, mainly because she'd picked up some unwelcome friends. Fleas. The pallet she'd been sleeping on, as well as Clem's pallet, seemed to be filled with the little monsters. Rachel killed a dozen or more, but finally gave up. There were just too many of them.

At sunup, Rachel and Rafe rode off Unaka Ridge. Maw and Zonie saw them off.

"We're beholden t' ye, Miss Rachel. You see her safe t'home, Rafe. You don't an' yore paw'll skin you alive!" Maw bellowed after them.

The ride home was hot and dull. Rafe silently led the way down tortuous trails visible only to him.

Rachel was too tired to care. She gave Star her head and dozed in the saddle.

"Hit's powerful hot. We best give these hyar hawses a drink."

Rafe's words jolted Rachel awake. They had stopped at the bank of a swift-flowing stream.

"That's a good idea," Rachel said, dismounting. "I could use a cool drink myself."

As she walked stiffly over to the creek and knelt to get a drink, Rachel could feel Rafe's eyes on her. His gaze made her feel naked.

"You shore air a purty little thang," Rafe said hoarsely. His eyes devoured the delicate curve of her back and her slender neck.

Rachel pretended not to hear him. Fear and anger swept through her. Instinctively, she realized both emotions would only spur Rafe on. With great difficulty, she held her temper down. The fear remained a cold lump in the pit of her stomach.

She calmly continued washing herself with the cool water. Her mind raced frantically. Could she overpower Rafe? No. Once he got his filthy hands on her, she had no chance. Outrun him? Rafe was between her and Star. Besides, he knew these hills and she didn't. Then what?

A warning from Granny Sharp popped into her head, "Be careful what you say and do. Many folks think us doctors are witches. They fear us, as much as respect us. Be careful never to make the witches' sign. Don't ever make a fist with your pinkie finger and your index finger sticking out. That's the sign of the Horned God. Witches used it to cast spells. So don't ever do it, if you don't want to scare the daylights out of someone."

It was worth a try!

Rachel rose carefully and turned to face Rafe who had silently moved closer to her. Her eyes looked coolly into his hot ones.

"Did you say something, Rafe?"

Rafe's gaze dropped to Rachel's outstretched right arm that was slowly moving toward him. The Horned God pointed straight at him. All the color drained from his face. The lust in his eyes turned to naked fear.

"N-no, ma'am, Miss Rachel. I-I never said nuthin'," Rafe stammered, backing away with a sick smile on his face.

"Must have been the wind talking," Rachel said, lowering her arm. "Sometimes it warns me of danger."

"Yes, ma'am," Rafe said respectfully. "We best git on, then. Maught be a bear around."

Rachel agreed and lept quickly into the saddle.

She didn't know whether to laugh or cry over her deception. The important thing was that it had worked.

Rafe would have had his way with her despite the swift and sure retribution by Grandy and his own Ma. That he was willing to chance. But he wasn't willing to take a chance on being hexed by a witch. It was almost funny. Almost.

At dusk, they came to the beginning of Carder property. Rafe reined in and allowed Rachel to move past him.

"Got no cash money to pay you. You tell Mister Carder there'll be a deer brung down fer ye come fall . . . and some frash honey."

"It'll be welcome. Good-bye, Rafe." Rachel gave Star her head and made for home—and a bath and food and normal folks.

"Leave the Crows to their nest! I don't ever want to go back there again," Rachel said to herself.

17

Rachel woke up happy for no apparent reason. She didn't examine her mood, for fear it would disappear.

The summer had been long and hectic, with only one letter from Ben. It had been only a short note from Virginia, saying he had rejoined his unit. Rachel had swung from dizzy, happy highs, in which she knew Ben would soon return, to deep, dark lows, in which she was certain he would be killed.

This morning, the last day of July, was one of Rachel's happy turns.

"I'm going out collecting herbs this morning," Rachel announced at breakfast.

"Good. Looks like a fine day for it," Manda replied, glad to see Rachel out of her blue spell for a while.

As Rachel mounted and rode off, her spirits soared and danced. She felt like bursting into song, only she didn't know one that would express how she felt. Instead she urged Star into a full gallop and tore off down the trail, her hair streaming behind her like a banner.

In a few minutes, she was racing along the creek by Uncle Roscoe's place. On impulse, she reined Star in and rode up to the cabin.

"Yoo-hoo! Aunt Rose—Jason!"

Aunt Rose came to the door. "Mornin', Rachel. What brings you out, lookin' so pert and chipper? Get down and set a spell."

"Morning, Aunt Rose. I just stopped by to see if Jason wanted to go herb gathering. Where is that sleepyhead?"

"He's beat you out. He rode off to town at daybreak. To see Hobie Hyder, he said. But I think maybe it was to see Hobie's cousin from Maryville. He's been to town twice since she came to visit."

"So, Jason's sparking a girl, is he? Well, I declare!"

"She'll either kill him or cure him," Aunt Rose said, laughing. "I told Jason he ought to stay in town with Mary Ann instead of all this ridin' back and forth. But he said he'd rather wear out a horse than listen to those squallin' young'uns of hers."

Clem Turner had spent less than a year in the War. He'd returned to run his place and to keep Mary Ann producing future farm hands. So far there were three little Turners and another on the way.

"Jason better get used to that music if he's serious," Rachel said, smiling. "What's this girl he's sparking like?"

"According to Jason, she's beautiful, kind, sweet, gentle, honest, lovable, and witty," Aunt Rose replied, smiling. "But I haven't seen her myself. She'll be coming to Meeting next Sunday, I reckon."

"Good. I'm dying to meet this absolutely perfect girl," Rachel said. "Jason deserves the best. So she'd better be all of those nice things and more."

"Funny you should say that," Aunt Rose replied.

159

"That's exactly what Jason said about Ben! Have you heard when Ben's coming back?"

"He's coming soon."

"Good. You heard from him then?"

"No. I just know he's coming soon. I feel it," Rachel replied, surprising even herself with her answer.

Aunt Rose smiled up at her. "I reckon you do, honey. You look happy as a meadowlark. Why don't you get down and have a cup of tea. I'm gettin' a crick in my neck looking up at you."

"I'd best get along. Thank you, anyway, Aunt Rose. If anyone comes looking for me, I'll be up around Sycamore Shoals gathering herbs or at Three Oaks just dreaming."

"I'll remember. I'll tell Jason you were by, too. I 'spect he's gonna want to tell you all about his new girl."

"He'd better! I'll see you at Meeting on Sunday."

Rachel spent a happy, carefree day gathering boneset leaves, nightshade, bloodroot, tizzy leaves, and pokeberries. It was good to be digging in the moist, rich earth. Good to be out in the warm sunshine under blue July skies.

Her herb gathering finished, she headed Star for Three Oaks. It had become her dreaming place, ever since Grandy had given it to her for her dowry the last night that Ben was here.

"Fine place to build you a home," Grandy had said. "Not too close to your folks and not too far away."

"It's perfect!" Rachel agreed, giving him a hug and kiss.

She and Ben had stayed up late into the night planning their new home.

Rachel turned Star loose to graze and ambled through the meadow up the hill. She sat down, resting her back against one of the oaks, and once again planned where every room in their house would go.

The Allen homeplace.

Ben said it would be a large house with at least six rooms, plus a surgery at one side for her.

Satisfied that at last she had everything just as she wanted it, Rachel relaxed and gazed over the distant mountains shimmering in the summer heat.

What kind of magical pull did they have?

She'd spent the first fourteen years of her life in towns and cities with other dreams and other ambitions. Yet those places and those dreams seemed like they'd happened to another person in another lifetime.

These mountains were her home, even if she never won full acceptance. It didn't matter quite so much, now that she had her doctoring and Ben. Their children—hers and Ben's—would be mountain born and bred. They would carry on this wonderful way of life in the very shadow of these mountains. It was a comforting knowledge.

Thinking about the future generations of Allens, Rachel's eyes grew heavy and she drifted into a pleasant sleep.

She awoke suddenly, with an eerie feeling that someone was watching her.

Rachel looked up to find Rafe Crow standing a few feet away, an evil grin on his unshaven face.

"Y'luk rat purty sleepin' thar," he said.

"Hello, Rafe," she managed to say calmly. "Is someone up your way sick again?"

"Nah. I'm hyar on m'own bizness," Rafe replied, with a low chuckle.

Rachel looked into his glinting blue eyes and felt fear.

"What business is that?" she asked, rising to her feet.

"I ben thankin' on yew sinct yew wuz up t' our place," Rafe replied hoarsely. "Maw sez if'n yew got a itch, scratch! I got me a itch. Onliest trouble be, I don't want no spell put on me! So's I went an' got me this."

Rafe held out a dirty rawhide bag toward Rachel.

"What's that?" Rachel asked, trying to back away. The tree blocked her retreat.

"Hit's a magic poshun. Long as I got this, yore spells won't work," Rafe said confidently, taking another step toward her.

In one swift flash Rachel's fear changed to anger. How dare this man destroy all her dreams! Her eyes flashed icy daggers at the leering Rafe.

"Are you certain of that, Rafe?"

"Certain sure! I done paid Widder Black dear fer it. Hit'll work."

Rachel clamped down on her blazing anger. It clouded her mind, so that she couldn't think.

"I don't want to hurt you, Rafe," she lied through clenched teeth.

Rafe chuckled. He liked a woman with grit in her craw.

"What cud a little bitty thang lak yew do t' me?" he asked playfully, sliding a step closer.

It was a good question. Rafe was bigger, faster, and stronger than she was. And the little rawhide bag robbed her of her one advantage over him—fear. A bluff was her only chance!

"Go home, Rafe!" Rachel commanded. "Go right now or I'll call up a spirit to crush you like a bug! Your rawhide bag is no protection from my magic."

Rachel's arm came up steady and firm with the witches' symbol pointed at Rafe.

Rafe hesitated. She sounded so sure of herself. A ripple of wind blew her skirt against her long, slender legs. His desire made him decide she was bluffing. Grinning wolfishly, he took another step.

A mere three feet separated them.

Rachel's nostrils flared at Rafe's pungent odor.

A disembodied voice boomed out of nowhere. "You called me, Mistress Rachel?"

Rafe stopped in midstep.

Rachel was too stunned to answer.

"Shall I crush his bones to powder?" asked the voice. "Or shall I burn him to a very small cinder? Command me, Mistress."

Rafe didn't wait for Rachel's reply. He dropped the rawhide bag and fled down the hill as if all the devils in hell were at his heels.

Rachel turned on wobbly legs to find the source of the voice.

Ben rose from the tall grass on the backside of the hill.

"Ben?"

Rachel closed her eyes tightly and opened them again. It was not a dream! Ben was striding toward her. She ran straight into his outstretched arms. They both began talking at once.

"When did you get here?"

"Who was that scoundrel?"

"How did you find me?"

"Aunt Rose told me where you were."

"I just knew you were coming soon!"

"I was trying to surprise you. I crept up the hill behind you and then I heard voices."

"Thank God, you're back safe!"

Ben put an end to their talk with a kiss.

Later, as they rode side by side back to Carder's Cove, Rachel asked quietly, "Ben, what would you have done if Rafe hadn't believed you were a spirit?"

Ben pulled a silver derringer out of his pocket. "I was all set to use this. Maybe I should have. Rafe Crow is a dangerous man."

"I'm glad you didn't. There's been enough bloodshed! Rafe won't bother me again. I saw his face when you spoke out."

"He'd better not!" Ben said grimly. "If I ever see him skulking around again, I will shoot him."

"It wasn't a very nice welcome for you. I'm sorry you had to see the worst side of us on your first day back," Rachel said sadly, as they rounded the bend in the river road.

"Even heaven had a fallen agel," Ben reminded her.

The setting sun threw long shadows over the people gathered around the porch of the Carder cabin.

A cheer went up as they rode into view.

Surprised, Rachel halted Bright Star. What were Aunt Rose, Uncle Roscoe, John, Andrew, Aunt Martha, Uncle Lem, Jason, Juner, two cousins, Grandy, and Manda doing here? Suddenly, Manda's words at Mary Ann's wedding came back to her. "It's the gathering of the clan!" she said to Ben through happy tears.

"The what?"

Rachel brushed her tears away. "Manda told me a long time ago that the clan always gathers to celebrate with one of its own. Don't you see, Ben? They have accepted both of us. Welcome home, Ben. Welcome back to our misty mountains."

AUTHOR'S NOTE

According to legend Miss Rachel still rides to tend her people. Some folks have even claimed to see Miss Rachel's ghost, mounted on her little strawberry roan, galloping over Unaka Ridge. Old-timers swear that if you hear the muffled tattoo of hooves drumming along the hollow, it is certain sure someone is sick up your way. They don't need a telephone, a CB radio, or a car to get news of a neighbor in trouble. All they need do is listen for Miss Rachel.

Once long ago I heard those ghostly hooves. In the morning I was told the story of Miss Rachel by our mountain hostess as she prepared our breakfast and a "sick" basket. I'm afraid I laughed at the superstition. I stopped laughing when a widow-lady with a broken hip was found up the hollow, some two miles away.

Whether or not the legend is true, it is true that Miss Rachel is fondly remembered by these proud, independent people who still live in the misty Appalachian mountains.